"Did you just see an empty boat floating in the middle of the ocean with the little girl in it?" Kelsey asked Ethan as she held the toddler close.

Ethan pulled out diapers and an extra outfit, very well-worn. Then he pulled out a card with a small handprint on it. He laid it on the table and stared at it.

"Ethan?"

"Ah...no. I didn't just find her. Someone sent me to the boat." His hands shook as he stared at a picture of an infant around six months old—and not of the little one Kelsey held.

"Ethan, who is that?" She gentled her voice. It was obvious the picture meant something to him.

He shook his head, his eyes on the photo.

Kelsey put her free hand over his, blocking his view. "Ethan, look at me. Who is the baby in the picture?"

He swallowed hard, his eyes dark with pain. "That picture is my son, Charlie. It was taken right before he died."

What was going on? Why would someone use this toddler to get to Ethan?

STEPHANIE NEWTON

penned her first suspense story—complete with illustrations—at the age of twelve, but didn't write seriously until her youngest child was in first grade. She lives in northwest Florida, where she gains inspiration from the sugar-white sand, aqua-blue-green water of the Gulf of Mexico, and the many unusual and interesting things you see when you live on the beach. You can find her most often enjoying the water with her family, or at their church, where her husband is the pastor. Visit Stephanie at her website, www.stephanienewton.net or send an email to newtonwriter@gmail.com.

THE BABY'S BODYGUARD

STEPHANIE NEWTON

Love Inspired

Recycling programs
for this product may
not exist in your area.

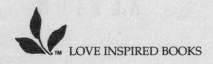 ™ LOVE INSPIRED BOOKS

ISBN-13: 978-0-373-44453-3

THE BABY'S BODYGUARD

Copyright © 2011 by Stephanie Newton

www.LoveInspiredBooks.com

Printed in U.S.A.

I will turn their mourning into joy and will comfort them and give them joy for their sorrow.

—*Jeremiah* 31:1

For Riley, who has the heart of a hero

PROLOGUE

Seven months of deep cover had led to this exact moment. The meet he'd been angling for since he'd hooked up with Antonio Cantori all those months ago. A direct line to the man who was pulling the strings behind a group of businessmen. Businessmen who bought and sold millions of dollars a week. And their sideline moneymaker—human trafficking, specifically little girls.

Ethan Clark picked up the satchel of money from the passenger side of his Jaguar sedan and looped it over his head. Once the money changed hands, he was done. A team of field agents would swarm the plush office behind the restaurant and take down the man pulling the strings. And Ethan could go home to his wife and baby.

The stakes were high, had never been higher. This was his last undercover assignment. He'd told his superiors at the FBI that he couldn't do this kind of operation any more. And the lives of those little girls were on the line, too. He'd held the weight of it in his heart for four long months, knowing he was powerless to save them.

But tonight was the night he changed things.

Ethan straightened his two-hundred-dollar tie and rounded the corner, pausing just for a minute to check out the gleaming windows of the Ristorante Giorgio, Cantori's place. His blood thrummed through his system. Adrenaline. Excitement.

A blonde pushing a baby stroller eased into view, walking toward the restaurant. He hesitated. She moved like his wife—like Amy—but it wouldn't be Amy. She didn't live in this town, didn't even know this place was on the map. He took a step closer. She stopped under a streetlamp, looked at her watch.

His wife. His baby.

Here?

Another step. She opened the door of the restaurant. She shouldn't be here. Shouldn't be anywhere close to here. But if he called out to her, his cover was blown and they were all dead. Amy, baby Charlie, and him.

The explosion slammed him against the building behind him. And when he opened his eyes, Amy was gone. The restaurant was a gaping, burning cave.

His mouth dropped open in a silent scream, his throat closing up on him so fast, he could barely whisper her name.

Sirens wailed and every car alarm in ten blocks blared.

"Amy."

Tony Cantori walked out of the wall of flames toward a vehicle waiting on the corner. His black eyes searched the block, passed Ethan and came back. He shaped his fingers into the sign of a handgun and made the motion of pulling the trigger at Ethan. Laughing, he jumped into a black van, which slid smoothly away from the curb.

Ethan ran for the restaurant, dropping the bag of money on the sidewalk. "Amy!"

He pushed through the crowd of people that had begun to gather outside. *"Amy!"*

Rough hands grabbed him, holding him back. He fought them. "I've got to get—my wife, my—"

New hands held his face. His partner, Bridges, made him hold eye contact. "You can't go in there."

Ethan bucked against the arms holding him back. His legs were restricted, but he surged forward, screaming. "Amy!"

Bridges grabbed him the way he would a child and held him. "It's no good, Ethan. They're gone."

His throat worked, tears locked against a wall of pain.

No.

ONE

Two years later

Ethan Clark had always preferred the gentle slap of water on a fishing boat to the raucous houseful of boys that he'd grown up in. He still had that old wooden fishing boat he'd inherited from his grandpa, but these days his ride was a dual-outboard powerboat fitted with blue lights.

Policing Florida's waterways kept Ethan Clark out of his house. Away from the memories. Away from concerned friends and relatives, from walls painted with cars and trucks—a room his little boy would never again sleep in.

His cell phone buzzed in his uniform pocket. He started to reach for it, but hesitated, his fingers curling into a fist. He'd been getting text messages for the last two weeks. Close-ups of a baby—a tiny foot, the curve of a cheek, a little hand, chubby and creased.

He had a trace put on the number, but it was untraceable—a throwaway cell phone. He slowed the boat to a troll, barely making waves, and opened his phone.

This time it wasn't a photo. It was geographical coordinates.

Ethan keyed the numbers into his onboard navigating system. It was his job to know the ocean well—and as the map popped up, he recognized this spot. Shallows about four miles out, half an hour from his location.

If the FWC—Florida's Fish and Wildlife service— had a plane in the area, they could scope it out from the air. He called in the coordinates and asked for aerial backup, really the only kind available on short notice out here.

He gunned the big engines on his boat, sending it plowing through the waves. Every stop, even the routine ones, had the potential for danger. A situation like this had all the earmarks of an ambush.

The radio squawked. "Marine Four, this is Eagle Two-ten. We've got eyes on that location. Looks like an abandoned boat. Over."

"Copy that, Eagle Two-ten. Thanks for the look-see. Over." *Abandoned* could mean a lot of things. Engine problems. Drugs. Crime scene.

Considering the text message directly to him, it definitely could mean the boat was set as some kind of trap. He had a lot of enemies from his time spent in the FBI. The fact that he'd laid low in the years since didn't mean squat. Some of those guys had extremely long memories.

"We'll circle until you're clear, Marine Four. Over."

"Roger. Marine Four out."

The boat in sight now, Ethan slowed his launch to a

crawl. Waves slapped against the bow, spraying arcs of salt water into the air. He trolled closer. Even through binoculars, he could see no movement on the anchored craft.

Flipping his speaker on, he announced his presence as law enforcement and his intention to board the craft.

Nothing. Not a sound, not a movement. The large pleasure cruiser rocked on its anchor with the motion of the waves.

Ethan cut his motor.

He dropped and set anchor in fast, efficient movements, prepping to board the other boat. Despite everything, he didn't have a death wish. Pulse thudding in his veins, he checked his sidearm, took a deep breath… and leaped.

The other boat rocked as he landed on the foredeck and braced his feet. He pulled his weapon and swung around toward the driver's position. Nothing. He blew out the breath he didn't realize he'd been holding.

Used to the roll and pitch of the ocean, he moved easily toward the stern, checking for signs of what might've happened here. There was no sign of struggle. Every cushion was in place. No scratches or scrapes marred the fiberglass surface of the deck.

Ethan heard a sound and whipped around. A little kid's sippy cup rolled in one corner of the otherwise completely empty boat.

A blue waterproof tarp covered one section of seats and the space underneath. Only one thing to do.

He jerked the tarp off.

Blue eyes blinked in the bright April sunlight. A tiny rosebud mouth opened wide to scream.

Ethan took a step back. He couldn't have been more flummoxed if he'd found a bomb under the tarp.

Instead he'd found a toddler.

Social worker Kelsey Rogers stood on the pier at the marina, her hair whipping in the early fall breeze. Her peasant blouse and capris were optimistic. She should've worn a coat, but like most everyone else in Florida, she preferred to pretend that the Sunshine State was always sunny and warm.

She dug in the pocket of her pants and pulled out her cherry ChapStick. Uncapping it, she slicked it on and shoved it back in her pocket. She'd gotten the emergency call an hour ago from the FWC. One of their law enforcement officers had found a baby abandoned at sea. Personally, she couldn't imagine it, but since she'd gone to work for the Department of Children and Families she'd seen a lot of things that she couldn't imagine parents ever doing to a child, so she tried not to have preconceived expectations.

She could see the flashing blue lights of the cop's boat long before she could actually see the occupants of the boat, but when he made the turn around the no-wake buoy into the marina, she caught her breath. Ethan Clark stood with his feet braced, one hand on the wheel, the other muscular arm around a curly-headed munchkin.

She'd met him once before on a search-and-rescue mission in a nearby state park. From what she'd seen, he was the strong, silent type. He commanded respect without saying a word.

Ethan cut the engine and glided in to bump gently against the posts of the pier. Even with the toddler firmly gripped in one arm, he still managed to toss Kelsey a line.

A worker from the marina, a young man around eighteen, came jogging down the dock. "Looks like you could use a hand."

Ethan tossed the teenager another line and within minutes had the big boat securely tied off to cleats on the pier.

He pulled aviator glasses off and tossed them onto the console in the middle of the boat. "Kelsey, thanks for coming down here."

"Wouldn't miss it. Hi, pumpkin. Wanna come to me?" She held her hands out for the baby as Ethan tried to disengage himself from the little arms. The child screeched and wrapped its arms tighter around Ethan's neck.

He shot her a what-now look.

"Maybe you should get out first—give the baby a chance to become familiar with me." She studied the tot in his arms. "A little girl?"

His blank look told her the answer to her question before he could. She grinned. "Well, she's wearing pink overalls, so I think it's a good guess."

"All I could really think about was getting uh, her, back to shore. It never crossed my mind to try to figure out a name or anything." Ethan stepped easily across the space between the boat and the pier, balancing not only his weight but the toddler's as well.

"Has she had anything to drink?" Kelsey dropped into step beside Ethan as he walked up the pier toward the marina sandwich shop.

"Yes, I carry water on board. I also gave her a few crackers." He shrugged. "I don't have much experience with kids."

The wind caught a piece of Kelsey's hair and tangled it around Ethan's arm. She laughed and stopped him with a hand on his arm.

He didn't move as she unwound the strand, his blue-gray eyes never leaving her face. The baby watched her, too, her little hands fisted in Ethan's uniform shirt.

She laughed again. "There. No harm done. I keep meaning to get it cut, but never have time."

Ethan took the few remaining steps to the sandwich shop and ducked inside. He dropped into a chair and re-arranged the little girl so she was sitting on his knee.

Kelsey pulled a chair out beside the two of them and dug around in her tapestry bag. A toy cell phone might break the ice. She pulled it out and punched a button, pretending to talk. "Hello? Oh, yes, you want to speak to Ethan. He's right here. Hold on a second."

She held the toy phone out to Ethan, who gave it the same look he might give a live grenade. She wiggled it at him. "Ethan? It's for you."

He took it from her hand and held it to his ear. "Uh-huh. Yeah, thanks. Okay, bye." He punched the red heart-shaped button and the phone played a silly song.

The baby loosened her grip on her shirt and lunged for the toy.

"She's small, but still—she looks seventeen or eighteen months old to me. Did you try talking to her?" Kelsey studied the little girl. Tangled blond curls bounced around the baby's cheeks.

"Just the basics. Name, rank, serial number."

Kelsey smiled. So there was a sense of humor in there. Somewhere.

"In fact, she looked at me like I was speaking a foreign language." He jiggled his knee like a pro.

"Hmm. Maybe you were. We've seen a lot of orphans from Eastern Europe in the last few years." She tapped the table to get the little girl's attention and said in Russian, "Hello, baby. Where's your mommy?"

No response. No reaction at all, in fact, from the baby.

Ethan was staring at her again, like she'd grown a second head. "Was that Russian?"

"Yeah, but she doesn't recognize it. It doesn't mean much, though. There are so many countries, and each one's language is just a little different."

"Where'd you learn Russian?" The toddler dropped the phone to the floor. Ethan picked it up, rubbed it on his pant leg, and handed it back to her.

"Russia." Pulling another toy out of her purse, a play remote control that made noise, she pushed the bright blue button. She reached her arms out to the baby, the toy in one hand. Without a second thought, the toddler threw herself into Kelsey's arms.

"Ha, success." She looked up to meet Ethan's steady

blue eyes. "I learned the language when I lived in Russia. My parents were missionaries. I've lived a lot of places."

She looked down at the baby and made a silly face.

Ethan smiled, but not a real smile, just a tilt of one corner of his mouth. It was a start, though. And without the baby holding on to him, she noticed something else. "What's that over your shoulder?"

He looked. "Forgot I picked it up. I guess it's a diaper bag."

"Do we need to wait for someone to look at it?" The toddler primped her mouth like she might cry, so Kelsey reached into the never-ending purse again and pulled out a bag of Goldfish crackers.

"Executive decision." Ethan unzipped the bag, his hands never faltering. He was so serious. So different from her. She bet he never wore flip-flops in the off-season.

He tilted up the side. "It has 'Jane' written in marker in the side of the bag. No birth date. Do you think that's her name?"

"We have to call you something, don't we, pumpkin?" Kelsey ruffled the little girl's curls. "Is your name Jane?"

The toddler grinned at her with a row of pearly baby teeth.

"Okay, then. We'll go with Janie." Kelsey handed her a cracker and popped one in her own mouth. "Did you just see an empty boat floating in the middle of the ocean with her in it?"

Ethan pulled out diapers and an extra outfit, very well-worn. Then he pulled out a card with a small hand-print on it. He laid it on the table and stared at it.

"Ethan?"

"Ah...no. I didn't just find her. Someone sent me to the boat."

His hands shook now as he turned over the photo-graph—a picture of an infant around six months old. It wasn't the one Kelsey held in her lap.

"Ethan, who is that?" Her voice grew gentler. It was obvious the picture meant something to him.

He shook his head, his eyes on the photo.

Kelsey put her free hand over his, blocking his view. "Ethan, look at me. Who is the baby in the picture?"

He swallowed hard, his eyes dark with pain. "That baby is my son, Charlie. It was taken right before he died."

Ethan shot to his feet. He couldn't figure out how this tiny blonde toddler figured into what happened to Charlie. What was going on? Why would someone use her to get to him? Why would they have him find her?

None of it made a bit of sense.

Kelsey pressed a drink into his hand. "Drink this. You need some sugar."

He looked down at her. "I'm fine. Just trying to figure out if I've missed something."

She hitched the little girl she'd been calling Janie higher on her hip. "Something tells me if we can figure out who this munchkin is we'll have another piece of the puzzle."

"You're right. It's been a while, but I should be able to get some information. I have some resources in law enforcement."

"When it comes to children, I have more. We'll find out what's going on." Her pretty brown eyes were unadorned with makeup, but they were determined.

Ethan believed her. He took a deep breath for the first time since he'd seen that photograph. Someone was messing with his head, enjoying yanking his chain. And he would get to the bottom of it.

His phone buzzed. He reached for it and felt Kelsey's soft hand on his arm. It felt like a lifeline.

He opened the phone to read the message.

Your son is alive.

TWO

Kelsey gripped Ethan's arm tighter as he swayed. "Ethan?"

He stared at the phone. She eased it from his cramped fingers and looked at the message. *Your son is alive.*

What in the world was going on? "Ethan, why don't we sit and you can tell me what happened to your son?"

He allowed Kelsey to lead him to the table. As he sat, the baby in her arms reached for him. With only a brief hesitation and something like deep pain settling in lines on his face, he took her. As Janie squirmed, he shifted her until she could lay her head on his shoulder.

Kelsey pushed the Coke toward him. "Okay, talk."

He met her eyes and to her surprise, she saw a hint of a smile there. "I think you're the only person who would have the nerve to ask me that. My family won't. I think they're afraid I'll go off the deep end."

"Is there danger of that?"

He rubbed a slow circle on the baby's back while he

seemed to be considering the question, and Kelsey's heart did a lazy flip in her chest.

"I don't think so." A rueful smile, then.

She smiled back at him, even though she wanted to cry, because there was courage, and then there was *courage*. He had the real thing. "Why don't you tell me about Charlie?"

Kelsey watched emotions—anger, fear, grief— travel across his face as he struggled to find the right words.

"I was undercover with the FBI. We were closing the deal with…some really bad people. All we needed was for the money to exchange hands and we could arrest them." He closed his eyes, almost as if he shut them tight enough he could shut out the memory of that night. "They shouldn't have been there. They shouldn't have known the place even existed. I wasn't anywhere near our hometown."

"Wait—your wife and son were at the place where the sting was set to happen?"

"Yes." The pain in that one word was enough to take her breath away.

"She walked across the street, right in front of me, and the restaurant where I was supposed to meet the people I'd been working to bring down…it just blew up. Amy and Charlie were killed in the explosion." He licked dry lips and took a sip of the Coke she'd opened for him.

"How did she get there?"

"No one was ever able to figure it out. There were some unexplained phone calls on the call log of her cell phone, but the numbers traced back to burn phones. I left the FBI, but if there were new leads, I'm sure they would have let me know." The toddler whimpered and roused. Ethan passed her to Kelsey, who lowered her into the crook of her arm and shushed her gently to sleep.

"You must feel like you've been living a nightmare that you can't wake up from."

His eyes took on a distant stare. The toll the last couple of years had taken on him had definitely been harsh. "You have no idea."

She did have an idea—not what it was like to lose a wife and child, but she had a very good idea what it was like to lose people you love. Family.

Living nightmares? That she had experienced.

"Ethan, how can you know if the message you got is for real? Is it possible that your son could've survived without you knowing?"

It wasn't possible. He'd watched as the explosion took his wife and child. And the small sliver of hope this message birthed in him only made the pain worse.

"No." He glanced at her, her question reminding him of her presence. "And I think I might know a way to prove it."

Ethan strode out the door of the marina shop with the photo in hand, Kelsey trailing behind with the toddler in her arms. The month before Amy and Charlie died, Ethan had been in Mobile for the weekend. A prearranged "business trip," which really meant a visit home for him.

He'd taken Charlie out for the afternoon to give Amy

won't take

a break. The two of them had gone to Kid's Day in the park. Cops and firefighters put it on so that kids could meet them, see their uniforms and the firefighters in their gear and learn not to be afraid.

At the event, the cops were fingerprinting and photographing kids, making identification kits. He had one made for Charlie. Amy had teased him about it, an ID kit for a six-month-old.

He'd put it away in a drawer and said they would never need it.

Ethan turned down the pier that led to his boat slip. He'd tried renting a house when he first moved back to Sea Breeze, but after everything that had happened, a house was too normal. And he needed the water. He bought his boat three months later.

Climbing on board, he held out a hand. She passed him the diaper bag and then, taking his hand, made the easy jump onto the stern of the boat. In the cabin, he had stowed a small wooden box that held the only pieces of his old life that he'd kept close.

He ran his fingers over the smooth wood. So many nights he took his box out of its storage space and held it. He didn't have to. He didn't need mementos to remember his son or his wife. They were engraved on his heart.

It was harder than he'd expected to open it.

"Do you want me to…" Kelsey's voice trailed off as she caught his expression.

"No, I can do it. It's just—"

"I get it. You don't have to explain." She laid the baby

on the berth and pushed a pillow under the mattress so Janie couldn't roll off.

He pulled the box closer and lifted the lid. Without allowing himself to think about it, he pulled out a silver baby rattle and the tiny T-shirt that Charlie wore on his first day of life. A pressed flower that his wife had kept from their first date. Other precious bits and pieces of a life gone by. And the fingerprint card and picture he'd made on the last outing he'd had with Charlie.

Laying the handprint beside the fingerprint card, he compared the two. Neither was very precise, considering they'd been done on a six-month-old. But he could see the swirls and arches. His heart began to pound.

They looked like a match, the newer one only slightly larger.

Kelsey pushed him out of the way and pulled the cards where she could see them. "Oh my—*Ethan*. They match."

He pushed away from the table and paced the dozen steps to the door of the cabin before turning back. "We need to get it verified."

"SBPD can do that. But I think the place for us to start is with her." She gestured to the little angel sleeping on Ethan's bunk. Janie's diaper-clad booty was hitched up in the air, and her chest rose and fell in even breaths. "If we find out who she is and who led her to you, just maybe that information leads to more information about your son."

Hope and desperation mixed inside him—the need to believe that it could be true, the desperate wish for something so improbable. He turned to pace the length of the boat again, but in the small space he quickly ran into Kelsey as she paced the other way.

He leaned against the wall, his stomach in knots. "I don't know what to think. We can try to trace her using the missing persons database, but something tells me she's not going to be there."

"I've got to get back to the office." Kelsey slung the diaper bag over one shoulder and picked the baby up, easily settling her on her shoulder without waking her. With one hand, she dug her cell phone out of the back pocket of her capris. "Put your information in my phone. If I find something I'll call you. With both of us working on this, something is bound to turn up."

After finishing out his workday—which was thankfully spent doing mundane work like stopping boats to check for onboard safety equipment—Ethan spent the entire night searching the internet for information. He'd turned the problem around in his head every way he could possibly think of, and still he came up with nothing. From grief to hope to frustration, he'd pretty much run the gamut.

And now, running on little sleep, he wanted to take someone down.

Someone like the criminals who had set this whole thing in motion in the first place. Who stole someone's child? Someone with no conscience. Someone who bought and sold people as commodities.

He slammed the brush on the surface of his boat and scrubbed. One thing about living on a boat—something always needed to be cleaned. Maybe it would help him work through some of his anger issues.

"Permission to come aboard, sir?" Kelsey's voice drifted out from the pier.

"Permission granted, but be prepared to swab the deck." Ethan reached for the T-shirt behind him on the rail and pulled it over his head.

"Nuh-uh. I've lived in Sea Breeze long enough to know better than to get between a man and his boat."

Despite himself, he laughed, turning to greet her. She was dressed in a simple khaki skirt and a T-shirt, but she had on several long necklaces of brightly colored beads, and Janie had her hands twisted up in them. "I thought she would be in foster care by now."

"It's always the goal to get kids placed as quickly as possible." Kelsey passed Ethan the baby and lightly stepped on board. "Unfortunately, all of our emergency foster care placements were full. We're on our way to the pediatrician for a checkup."

Janie grabbed his face and grinned, a half-dozen teeth on the top and bottom shining in her mouth. "She looks pretty happy."

"I think she's doing fine. I came by because, as I was looking through her diaper bag this morning, I found this." She handed him an SD card, the kind that would go in a digital camera. "I don't know what's on it, but I thought it might be more evidence. It was sewn into the lining of her bag."

Ethan stuffed the card into one of the pockets of his cargo shorts, one of the pockets that wasn't wet from scrubbing the deck. Janie bounced on his free arm, but as she bounced, her foot got caught in his pocket.

She bounced again, but her foot didn't come loose. Her face mashed up into a red-faced scowl. A wail came out of her mouth that rivaled the air horn he carried on his boat for emergencies. He hadn't known she could do that. He looked at Kelsey. "A little help here?"

Kelsey loosened Janie's foot, but stepped away, leaving him to deal. She dug in the diaper bag. He patted the baby on the back and shushed and—what was that other thing he'd read in the baby book you were supposed to do with crying kids?

His natural calm disappeared as she wailed. It was forever ago that he'd done baby stuff. *Think, Clark. You've got this.*

He started rocking back and forth. Yeah, that was it, *motion.*

It didn't work, not even for a second.

Janie didn't stop crying, but she did hiccup and gasp as she cried. Screaming kids made all kinds of crazy noises, but she didn't sound right. He laid her back on his arm to look at her. Her lips were blue. "Kels—"

Kelsey came up with a sippy cup and a scrap of a blanket from the diaper bag.

"I don't think that's it. There's something wrong with her. She's blue—look at her hands." His voice had risen, and he felt something close to panic.

"What?" Kelsey dropped the bag onto the deck. "Let me see."

Janie hadn't stopped crying, and her breathing was

fast and shallow—not wheezing, like asthma, but as if she was trying to get more oxygen.

"Call 911." Ethan might be calm on the outside, but inside he was freaking out. *Oh, Jesus, please protect this little baby.*

"Wait just a minute." Kelsey took Janie from Ethan and held her close, letting her have the blanket, which didn't really work. She didn't even notice it. But then she tucked Janie's legs up, almost against her own little armpits and held her close against her chest, rocking and singing to her—in Russian, he guessed.

Slowly, the baby calmed and began to suck her thumb. Her color returned, not quite pink, but not grayish-blue either. He picked up her little hand. The nails still had a bluish tinge, but the hands weren't blue. His own heart rate started to return to something resembling normal.

"Russian?"

Kelsey nodded. "I don't think it's her language because she doesn't really respond, but it probably sounds a lot more familiar to her than English."

He dropped onto a bench seat. "I was afraid she was going to die. How did you know to do that?"

"I didn't know, not for sure." She eased to the seat beside him. Janie's eyes were drifting shut, but her color was good. Crisis averted, for now. "But kids in underdeveloped countries don't have the kind of medical care we have here, so I've seen this before. I think it's a heart defect."

"Oh, right—missionary kid. Where was this?" He

heart Bigt

watched Janie's chest rise and fall, not quite ready to assume she was going to be okay.

"Rwanda. There was a little kid there who would be running and playing and then all of a sudden his lips and hands would turn blue and he would gasp for air, just like this. His fix was to stop and squat down and lean forward. It's a crude treatment, but it works—for a while." She stood with the baby in her arms. "I think instead of going straight to the pediatrician, I'll have the pediatrician call Children's Hospital. She needs to be seen by a specialist."

He grabbed the diaper bag and sippy cup from the deck and followed her toward her car. "Do you want me to go?"

"We'll be fine. I'll keep you posted when I can."

Seven hours later, Kelsey pulled up at the drive through at Chick-fil-A. She briefly felt guilty about her choice, but just as quickly discarded the thought. She was starving. And she was traumatized.

Janie had been poked, prodded, stuck, ultrasounded, echoed and basically put through every test any of the pediatric cardiologists could think of at the children's clinic. And every test came back with the same result. She was one sick little baby. The miracle, they said, was that she had lived—and basically thrived—this long. She was small for her age because of the lack of oxygen and nutrients getting to her cells.

And she would have to have surgery as soon as the doctors could arrange it. Normally kids with her condition would've had surgery before they were a year old.

The thought that this little baby might've died because no one had gotten her the medical treatment she needed…Kelsey took a deep, cleansing breath and tried not to focus on how angry it made her.

The perky teenager handed Kelsey a bag of yummy chicken and fries and not one but two milk shakes. She figured if she was going to go bug Ethan, she should at least take a food offering.

She hadn't really stopped to think why she was going to him. Maybe it was because he had found Janie, and she thought maybe he would have an emotional connection. Maybe it was because she saw how tender he was with the baby. Or how worried he'd been when she had had the episode earlier this morning.

He was someone she admired, someone she was working with. That was all. Maybe it was the fact that, like her, he'd endured more than anyone should have to. The fact that his beautiful blue eyes connected with hers in a way that she'd rarely felt before…well, that was just something she would have to deal with.

He needed to find his son. She needed to find out the identity of the baby currently sleeping in the backseat of her car.

They could help each other.

She passed the turn to her house and kept going to the marina. When she pulled into a parking place, she called his phone. When he answered, his deep voice, raspy from lack of use, rumbled in her ear.

"Hi, I'm in the parking lot. I have news."

"Be right there."

In two minutes, he came walking down the pier, a computer under his arm, his long, jean-clad legs eating up the distance. He slid into the passenger seat, glanced in the backseat at the sleeping baby and then back at her, those blue eyes full of concern. "Is she okay?"

"She will be." Kelsey handed him a milk shake. He looked at it like it was a bomb. "It's chocolate. Drink it."

He took a sip. "What did the doctor say?"

"Doctors, plural. We just got done. She has to have surgery. Maybe more than one. Tetralogy of Fallot is the genetic defect that causes her to turn blue, but she also has another defect that has to be repaired. It turns out it's pretty rare."

"Wherever you have to go, we can take her."

Here he was, his son missing after two years of being presumed dead, and he was offering to take her wherever she needed to go, whatever she needed to do to take care of Janie.

It was enough to melt the strongest woman's defenses, and she was a sucker for a soft-hearted man.

Kelsey took a long sip of her milk shake and cleared her throat. "There is some good news, though. The pediatric cardiologist at Children's emailed the records for Janie to the specialist in Boston and got him on the phone. It seems that this doctor has been emailed her records before."

Ethan jolted. "So we can identify her?"

"Maybe." This was the frustrating part, the part that had her banging her head on a wall for most of the afternoon. Well, more than the constant waiting with a fussy baby. "The doctor wouldn't release the records he had. In fact, he wouldn't reveal any information about her at all, not even the doctor who originally emailed the records."

"We need to get a court order. That's the closest thing to a lead I've seen. I have someone I can call—"

She shook her head, smiled. "I'm already on it. There's a federal judge here who knows a judge in the Boston area he can tap for a warrant. I called him this afternoon when it became clear that Boston was going to be difficult."

Ethan turned to her, and there was the smile, just that little tug, at the corner of his mouth. "Oh, you *are* good."

"It isn't my first time around this particular block with doctors and records on foster children. I go straight for the big guns. So what did you find out?"

In answer, he opened his computer and clicked through to the photo gallery. At least a hundred, maybe two hundred photos of infant faces popped up.

She sucked in a breath. "All those are…?"

Ethan shrugged. "Without any more information, I can only assume that they are babies who were trafficked here for profit. Adoption scam is what I'd guess. There's a lot of money to be made if the person is ruthless enough." He clicked on one about halfway down. "Here's Janie."

"She would've been an adoption risk because of her birth defect. If anyone made a stink, they would put the whole operation in jeopardy."

"Exactly. This one—" he scrolled up a little bit and his cursor hovered over another picture "—is my son. It looks like it was taken about two weeks to a month after he supposedly died. I think this is proof that he was abducted."

"That's absolutely incredible."

He nodded. "I don't know what Amy was doing at the restaurant that night, but at least now I can figure that it had something to do with these babies being trafficked and Charlie being kidnapped."

Kelsey reached for his hand. "I'm so sorry, Ethan."

His gaze tracked to meet hers. And held.

"I know." He took a long, slow breath and opened the door. "Do you want me to follow you home?"

How could he be worried about them when he was the one who'd just heard life-altering news? News that turned the belief he'd had for the last two years on its head. It had to be killing him that his son could be alive, yet he didn't know where he was.

She shook her head. "We'll be all right. I just live a few blocks away. We're almost neighbors."

"Okay, I'll check in with you tomorrow."

She thought he would slam the door because most people wouldn't consider the sleeping child in the backseat. But not Ethan. He closed the door gently.

She pulled out of the parking lot and headed toward her house. Ethan stood alone in the parking lot, his hand raised in farewell. After all these years in the mission field, saying goodbye was a particular talent of hers.

It seemed that Ethan was pretty good at it, too.

THREE

When they were partners, Ethan wouldn't have waited to call Bridges. If he hadn't been able to sleep because of the puzzle of evidence crowding his head, he would've called him in the middle of the night, or in the early hours of the morning. New information would've meant an instant call, day or night.

But he and Bridges hadn't been partners in more than two years.

Ethan hadn't even talked to his former partner in close to nine months. Without the day-to-day working relationship and with the secret nature of the job that Bridges did, there wasn't as much as Ethan would've thought to build a friendship on. And truthfully, at the time, Ethan hadn't cared.

Now he needed help to put together the random pieces of this case. Because of the trauma surrounding the event, there were things Ethan didn't remember about the night Amy died. Hopefully Bridges could put those things in place.

The voice was grumpy and sleep-thickened, but sounded the same. "Bridges."

"Still aren't checking caller ID, I see."

"Ethan Clark. You better have a good reason for waking me up at one in the morning, my friend."

"It can wait until tomorrow."

"No, I'm awake. What's going on?" Sleep had disappeared from Bridges' voice. A field agent got used to being awakened in the middle of the night. Ethan waited for the twinge, the little giveaway that he missed the job he used to do in the FBI when he was partners with Bridges. It wasn't there.

With concise, short sentences, Ethan filled in his former partner on what had happened in the last two days, only leaving the fact that he believed his son might still be alive. "I just can't figure out how all this ties in to what we were working back then or why someone would reach out to me now."

Bridges was silent on the line. Then, "Ethan, you have to know that we searched every piece of ash from that explosion. There was nothing. Cantori was smoke, like he'd never existed."

"I know." The knot in his stomach was back. He dug in his pocket to find the roll of Tums he'd bought at the convenience store earlier and thumbed off a couple. "What about the girls?"

"We never found where he was keeping them. The only thing I could ever figure is that the operation is tight, with only a few key players. You know that— you're the one who was in with them."

It was true. "What about your confidential informant?"

"You don't remember?"

The question he'd been dreading. And because Booth Bridges had been his partner, he had to be honest. "Everything is hazy, Booth. I tried to wipe it all out of my memory for two years."

There was silence on the line. Then his former partner cleared his throat. "The CI was killed in a car accident a few weeks after you went in. The wreck was cleared by local cops as accidental, but neither of us thought it was an accident."

Ethan had a vague recollection. "He was eliminated."

"Yes, I think so." Bridges sighed heavily. "We can't protect you, Ethan."

"What are you saying?"

"I'm saying that these are very dangerous players. If you open this back up, you'll need to watch your back. These guys—they play for keeps."

Anger roared through Ethan. Deftly, with the familiarity of long practice, he pushed it back, though his voice shook with the effort. "I think I'm in a position to be aware of that."

His partner's breath came across the line in a rush. "Of course you are. I wasn't thinking. I'm sorry, Ethan."

"Even if I had nothing personally at stake, I don't know how I could let this go. If they are selling babies, then there's a lot more to this than we realized. More than a simple trafficking-for-profit scheme." As if that wasn't bad enough. His lip twitched. Frustration. Anger again.

Like an echo of his own feelings, frustration came through the line in his former partner's voice, as well.

"Right now all you have is an unidentified child, and I'm not sure what you want me to do with that."

"We're handling it. Local P.D. are on it and the FBI out of Mobile is involved in her case. What I need is information about the case that we worked. If it wasn't about selling those young girls, what was it about?"

The line went quiet. Ethan could hear the clink of ice falling into a glass and liquid splashing in after it. Then, "For years, we've been going at this from the angle of trafficking women and coming up with nothing. Maybe I can run this new information by someone at Crimes Against Children and see if I turn up any complaints. It's a stretch, but I'll try."

"That's all I can ask." Ethan stared into the darkness at the lights on the opposite shore. "Thanks, Booth. I owe you one."

"No. I don't think you do. I think we all owe you, Ethan."

Stuffing the sigh down, Ethan said, "Keep in touch," and as Bridges hung up on his end of the conversation, he resisted the urge to throw the phone. He hated feeling like he'd just been dealt the pity card, but if Bridges wanted to follow this through out of some misguided sense of a debt owed, so be it.

At least he would see where it led.

A few blocks away, Kelsey laid a very sleepy baby into the porta-crib. Janie's golden curls were still damp from the bath, and she sighed in her sleep, her mouth moving just a touch, like she missed her thumb. Too cute.

The doctor had said that she needed surgery as soon as possible, maybe as soon as next week, to put a shunt in her heart, giving her time to grow until they could do the full reconstructive surgery. She was trying to find the right doctor to follow Janie's care here in Florida. The red tape to get an unidentified child transferred from one state to another for state-funded medical care was going to be difficult—actually, she wasn't sure it had ever been done. But Janie deserved a bright future. In the meantime, Kelsey would be vigilant and try to keep her as calm as possible.

She gave the baby's back one last pat and turned toward the bathroom. Seeing and interacting with multiple children on a daily basis was one thing, but caring for a toddler minute by minute was exhausting—especially after the day they'd had at Children's Hospital.

They were close to finding out who Janie really was, though. Closer than Kelsey had imagined they would be at this point, thanks to the medical records. She squeezed toothpaste on her toothbrush and reached for the water, turning it on and quickly off again as she thought she heard the sound of something outside.

Her heartbeat picked up speed. She didn't hear it again. Maybe it was just her imagination. Or an animal in the trash cans. Maybe he hadn't found anything to his tastes, so he'd ambled on to check someone else's garbage. She resisted the urge to check under her bed for the baseball bat she kept. She didn't have to—she knew it was there.

She turned the water on again, straining her ears

Prayer

to listen as she brushed her teeth. Glass broke and she swallowed a mouthful of toothpaste.

That hadn't been her imagination.

That sound had been in her kitchen. Her legs were quaking, blood rushing in her ears. She ran for the bedroom door and closed and locked it silently, flipping off the lights at the same time.

Now what? Did she stay and take her chances on the police getting there in time? She felt her way across the room to her bedside table, finding her cell phone and stuffing it in the pocket of her sweatpants.

She grabbed the bat from under the bed. Hovering over the baby's crib, she considered her options.

Stay and hide. Pray the baby doesn't cry.

Make a run for it out the patio door.

The safety of the baby was her first priority. And if she stayed in the house with an intruder, the baby would be at risk. But what if someone had waited outside?

She breathed a prayer, one she'd said since childhood. *Please God, go before us and behind us. Guard us and protect us.*

Kelsey heard a door open down the hall. There really was someone in her house. Nausea burned in her stomach. She had to make a decision.

Coming closer. *Oh, dear God, help.*

Janie's new medicine was in the diaper bag. She grabbed it off the floor and threw it over her shoulder. She had to leave now, if she was going to. Making the decision, she put the bat down and lifted Janie from the crib. *Don't wake up, don't wake up.*

She crept to the glass doors, her legs weak, the

baby's weight heavy in her shaking arms. Her breath was coming in quick gasps. She had to calm down and think.

From the vantage point in here, the patio looked clear. If she went straight out the back without being seen, she could cut through the neighbor's yard and be at Ethan's boat in less than five minutes. She had to get out without being noticed. The night was dark, no moon to speak of. If she didn't make noise, if the baby was quiet. If the intruders were busy in the house.

So many ifs. She had to take the chance, though. Janie's safety, her safety, depended on it.

Now or never. Her heart pounding loud enough to wake the baby on its own, she flipped the lock, slid the glass doors open and stepped out, silent in her bare feet.

Don't wake up, don't wake up.

She ran.

The slate pavers on her patio cut into her feet, but she didn't slow down or cry out. She had to get through the trees to the street behind her house. Holding Janie close to her chest, she thumbed the two on her phone, where she'd programmed Ethan's number. As it rang, she heard a shout from behind her. From her house. "Oh, no. No, no, no. Do not follow me."

Janie lifted her head. "It's okay, sweetie, go back to sleep."

"Ethan Clark."

Relief flooded her at the sound of his voice, but he was still so far away. "Ethan, someone—in my—house. I ran. I'm not sure—I think—they followed."

"What? Where are you?"

She had to stop for a second. She had to breathe. Flattening herself against the fence in the neighbor's yard, she glanced back at her house. A light flashed in the window. A flashlight?

The door slammed open and she heard more shouting.

She whispered urgently into the phone. *"They're coming!"* She ran. The marina was about four blocks from here, but she was on the street now. She could run faster. She hitched the baby up in her arms. Janie whimpered but didn't cry.

Her pursuers crashed through the bushes in her neighbor's yard half a block away.

She tried to glance back to see where they were, stumbled and nearly went to her knees. Her cell phone skidded to the curb. She left it.

One wish. One prayer. *Safety.*

Something whizzed past her ear and she heard a metallic thud in the mailbox closest to her. Was that…oh, no, it *was*. They were *shooting* at her.

Help.

It was as close to a prayer as she could get, especially when she had a few choice words she'd like to say to the people shooting at a *baby*.

A shout came from in front of her. "Kelsey, run for the boat!"

She didn't hesitate. Here was help.

Ethan didn't hear a gunshot, but he saw the muzzle flash and heard the metallic thud as the round hit a mailbox feet from where Kelsey ran with the baby. Silenced weapon, which meant professional.

That Kelsey had been able to escape at all was pure miracle.

From somewhere he pulled calm, clear thinking. He put a bullet in the ground near where he'd seen muzzle flash. Another into the bushes. He heard a muffled cry.

All he needed was to keep the gunmen busy long enough to give Kelsey time to get safely on the boat.

A baby's wail lifted on the air.

The calm disappeared. Someone had sent killers after an innocent woman and child, and not for the first time. Anger spilled into rage. He fired another shot toward the bushes.

"Ethan, we're on board." Kelsey's voice came to him from the boat as a silenced shot hit the pole next to him, showering splinters of wood.

The weapon the hitmen were using was made for close-quarters hits, not the distance shots they were taking, but the impact of the bullets was too close for comfort.

He ran for the boat.

He had it idling already, but the lines were still attached to the pier. He turned and fired behind him at the bushes again, where at least one of the gunmen was hiding.

Ethan threw the bowline into the boat, and as he ran for the stern, he saw Kelsey pulling in the stern line. "Good girl."

He jumped on board as she cleared the line and

followed, ducking as another shot slammed into the tower. "Baby?"

"Safe below."

"Get down there with her. You need to be under cover." Ethan climbed the tower to the bridge and pushed the throttle slowly forward, easing out of the slip. As he cleared the pilings, a round hit the GPS, blowing it to smithereens.

He took a deep breath.

In the harbor area, he was the law. And the law said no-wake. He consoled himself with the thought, as he slammed the throttle forward, that not even he would write a ticket for someone speeding away from a professional hitman.

The lights of the marina faded quickly into the distance. He wouldn't take a bet that the hitmen would do the same. If they were hired to do a job, they wouldn't quit until it was done. He was going to need help keeping Kelsey and Janie safe.

As they traveled deeper into the bay, the night settled heavy around them. Safe—for now.

He slowed the boat to a stop and sat, letting his heart rate settle, letting his thoughts settle. The night sounds of the bay were as familiar to him as his own heartbeat. The song of the frogs in the estuary, the soft slap of the water against the side of the boat, the deep growl of a gator somewhere off in the distance.

He flicked a piece of glass off the bridge—what remained of his GPS. It didn't matter. He didn't need it to know where he was in this body of water. He took a deep breath for the first time in what seemed like hours.

"All clear?" Kelsey's soft voice was laced with exhaustion.

Ethan dropped down the ladder to the deck below. "For now."

She wrapped her arms around his waist and held on, resting her head on his chest, her long hair falling out of its clasp to slide against his skin. The smell of sweet herbs drifted up from the strands. "I was so scared."

He held on to her, just held on. It had been so long since he'd been held by another person. Since he'd held someone. He'd forgotten what it was like.

Ethan patted her back, much the way he would Janie's. And found a creeping sense of peace that he didn't expect. He closed his eyes, letting the night sounds and the feel of her in his arms give him rest.

She sniffed and moved a half step back. It was dark, but he could still see her eyes, searching out his. "I prayed for help. And there you were."

"I don't think there was anything miraculous about it, Kels—I was just here." He didn't want to step away from her; he wanted to fix this. He wanted to hold her again. Feel her hair against his chin, her head against his chest, feel that sense of belonging when he'd felt like a piece of driftwood for the last two years.

But he didn't take her back in his arms.

It wasn't that he felt unfaithful, exactly. Just weird.

She walked to the deck rail and looked out. "Prayers don't always get answered, not like that. Not even just in the nick of time."

He knew about unanswered prayers, and he wondered when it was that her prayers had gone unanswered, wondered if he should ask. But he settled for, "I know."

He'd been praying for guidance and protection for his son. That they would find him. But how did he learn to trust in God again? How had she?

"I guess you do." She didn't look at him. "And I'm sorry for it." Shaking the mood, she turned back. "So what now?"

Ethan didn't hesitate. This was a question he knew the answer to. "Now we get you somewhere we can keep you safe. Both of you. Somewhere with high walls and high-tech security. I know just the place. It won't be long."

He climbed the ladder to the bridge and started moving the boat forward, but his thoughts—those were with a black-haired social worker down below. One with a heart the size of the Gulf of Mexico and shadows that came into her eyes once in a while.

High walls and high-tech security, he'd told her. He hadn't mentioned the team of highly trained security specialists his brother and his wife had staying on holiday at their bed-and-breakfast, Restoration Cove. If anyone could keep her safe, they could.

He just hoped it would be enough.

FOUR

Kelsey held Janie close, peering out at their destination as Ethan let the boat glide into the pier. Lights gleamed from the windows of a gigantic house. Where had he brought her?

She heard his feet hit the deck after quick footsteps down the ladder. He tossed a line from the stern of the boat to a man waiting on the dock, all practiced, efficient motion.

When the bowline was tied off as well, Ethan met the man in the stern of the boat. A clasped hand, a bumped shoulder—they murmured an exchange that she couldn't hear, but it was clear the man wasn't a stranger to Ethan.

He turned to the door where Kelsey waited. "Kelsey, this is my brother, Tyler. And this is Restoration Cove."

The baby was sleeping, so Kelsey nodded as she stepped closer. Ethan's brother looked like him, but darker. Darker hair, darker eyes.

Tyler put a hand on her back as the boat rocked. "My wife, Gracie, is waiting for you in the kitchen at the main house. She has a room ready for you." When she hesitated, he smiled. "It's okay. We'll be right behind you."

Ethan made a sound of protest.

"She's safe here, Ethan," Tyler said softly. With his hand on Kelsey's elbow, he helped her forward before turning back to his brother.

She walked down the long dock toward the shore, looking back only once as she felt Ethan's eyes on her. He was deep in conversation with his brother, but he watched her.

Ethan had suffered a huge loss, one he was still reeling from. And yet he wanted to protect her. He wouldn't have brought her here if he hadn't thought it was the safest place for them.

As she got closer to the main house, she realized it was huge. A mansion. The door flew open, spilling light onto the marble terrace. A blonde in cropped sweatpants, an SBPD T-shirt and flip-flops stood in the door.

Janie stirred in Kelsey's arms, but despite the events of the evening and all the moving, she settled back to sleep.

"I'm Ethan's sister-in-law, Gracie. Come on in. I put a porta-crib in one of the guest rooms. My husband picked the room. It's not the nicest—there's no balcony—but it is roomy, and apparently, sniper-proof."

At Kelsey's quick, wide-eyed look, Gracie stopped in the middle of the hall. "I'm sorry. I'm so used to the law enforcement types we get around here. I forget you're a layperson."

"You're not?"

Gracie started up the stairs. "Not really. I'm a forensic psychologist, or was, until Tyler and I opened Restoration Cove. I still work on call with the Crisis Response Team as a hostage negotiator." She pushed open the door to one of the guest rooms. "And I work as a counselor here."

Kelsey walked into the room. As Gracie had said, there was plenty of space for the porta-crib, which had been placed on the wall closest to the hall. The headboard of the bed was upholstered in a pale blue-and-brown scroll print. The fluffy white comforter had a cornflower-blue throw casually tossed at the end that, at first glance, Kelsey was pretty sure was cashmere.

"You do have your own bathroom," Gracie said softly, as she gestured to a door at the opposite end of the room.

Soft light shone from the lamp on the desk angled into a corner. It was beautiful and cozy without being girly. Luxurious and understated.

Kelsey gently laid the toddler in the crib. Janie opened her eyes and blinked, saw Kelsey, and smiled. Oh, boy. If she really woke up now, they were in for an all-nighter. Kelsey laid the tattered piece of blankie next to Janie's face and patted her on the back. With a sigh, the toddler rolled over on her tummy and tucked the blankie under her chin, her eyes fluttering shut again.

With every child Kelsey rescued from a dangerous situation, she felt a tug on her heart. A responsibility that went beyond just a job. She had defenses, of course—she had to or she wouldn't be able to do her job at all.

But this little girl, all sixteen point two pounds of her, had wormed right under those defenses in about ten seconds flat.

Gracie waited at the door. Kelsey turned to her, tucking one bare foot behind the other, aware her appearance didn't quite measure up to her surroundings.

"You've had a tough day." Gracie's eyes were kind, and without warning Kelsey's burned with tears.

She pressed her fingers to them. "You have no idea."

"Believe me, I know how it feels. Come on, I'll give you the nickel tour, and if you like, we can join the guys for some tea."

As they left the room, Gracie closed the door behind Kelsey. "Don't worry about her. She'll be fine. We have great security here."

"That's what Tyler said. Why?" She followed Gracie down the hall to another door, which opened into a small sitting room.

"The real reason is that last year my sister tried to kill me." Gracie looked back at Kelsey and rolled her eyes. "Try to say that without freaking somebody out. We had the security system put in after that, and since then, we've upgraded."

She let Kelsey walk into the room before her. "We're a bed-and-breakfast, as you can tell, but we have a special mission. We cater to law enforcement officers and agents and their families who need a place to rest and recover."

"I've never heard of anything like it before."

"When Tyler came out of the DEA, he needed a place to figure out life. The Cove did that for him. We figured maybe it could be that for other people too. We have all the amenities of a high-end resort, but we also have counseling services available for those who request it. And occasionally, we provide a safe house if there's a need." Gracie dropped into a chair and curled her feet underneath her. "Like I said, we have excellent security."

"Thank you for taking us in." Kelsey sank into a comfy wide sofa and dropped her head into her hands. "It's not the first time I've been under attack by armed gunmen, but I certainly didn't expect it in my own home."

"No one ever expects violence. What happened the last time? Was it another case?"

Life had taught Kelsey at an early age to roll with the punches, put the past behind you. She'd had to, to survive. The attack on her village in Rwanda wasn't something she talked about—ever. She was obviously more affected by the events of today than she thought, for that event to be up front, right there, in her mind. "It was a long time ago. I lived overseas with my parents. Things are different in third-world countries."

She slanted a look at Gracie, whose blue eyes didn't miss anything.

"If you want to talk about it, that's literally what I'm here for. Sometimes it helps to talk." A wry smile curved Gracie's lips. "And, according to Tyler, sometimes it helps to beat the living daylights out of something. He leads a hand-to-hand combat class on the back lawn every morning. Because I insist, we also have tai chi on the beach at sunset. You know you're welcome here, Kelsey."

Kelsey drew in a deep breath. "You have no idea how grateful I am."

"I think I do." Gracie unfolded herself from the chair and gestured to a different door from the one they came in. "That door also leads back to your room. Since you have the baby, you should consider this room as part of your personal space. I'm going to check on the men and head back to my quarters. We do have guests at the moment, so I'll be back here in a couple of hours to help Tyler with breakfast."

"Thanks." Kelsey stood, hugging Gracie. The same early life lessons that had taught her to roll with the punches and put the past behind her had taught her to show affection when she felt it. She'd learned she might not have another chance.

Gracie squeezed. "I'll see you in the morning. Sleep as late as you want. I'll save you something." ·

A laugh snorted out. "Oh, I wish. Janie has—for the most part—slept through all the excitement tonight. I have a feeling she'll be up in time to help Tyler with the pancakes."

At the door, Gracie turned back, blond curls bouncing around her shoulders. "Oh, I figured you left in a hurry, so there are a few things for you in the dresser."

Gracie left the door open. Kelsey laid her head on the oversized arm of the sofa. Tyler and Gracie had both said she was safe here, that Janie was safe here. What an amazing feeling, to be able to relax her guard, even for just a few minutes.

She closed her eyes. Today had been such a long day and she was so very tired. Maybe she would rest just a minute before she went to find those clothes.

The smell of bacon and coffee roused Ethan from the small bit of restless sleep he'd managed. His brother had fired questions at him for over an hour about what had happened, how they would keep Kelsey safe and what they would need to accomplish it. He'd walked out on Tyler once the police called and said they had evidence that at least one of the hitmen had been injured. Lots of bullet holes, but no casings. These guys were definitely professionals.

All the while he'd kept turning the mystery over and over in his mind. Who took his child? And how had they managed it right under the noses of his team and left virtually no trace?

Who had left a tiny toddler—a sick one, no less— alone in a boat for him to find, along with the information about his son? He wondered about the intentions of the person who would do such a thing. Could they possibly be good?

Obviously he was now on the search for his son, and Janie would get the medical care that she needed. He still couldn't understand why he or she would go to such lengths to get his attention. Surely a meeting at a coffeehouse would've worked just as well.

There were too many questions. Too little information. He might be stuck here, but that didn't mean he didn't have goals—to find his son and close a case that was apparently putting them all at risk.

Charlie was the one thing he hadn't talked with Tyler about last night. It wasn't that he didn't think Tyler would believe…maybe he just wanted to keep it close to his heart for a little while longer.

His phone buzzed in his back pocket. He pulled it out and looked at the readout. Restricted number.

A sense of excitement mixed with foreboding as he pushed the send button. "Clark."

"Ethan Clark?" The voice raised the hair on his arms. He knew this voice. The last time he'd heard it was on the phone, making the arrangements for the day on the night his wife was murdered.

His lip twitched involuntarily. "Hello, Cantori."

"Well, of course, I don't go by that name now, but it will do for these purposes."

"How did you get this number?" Ethan didn't think he could manage a civil conversation much longer.

"A mutual friend gave it to me."

Ethan's fingers went cold. Who had he talked to that had talked to Tony Cantori? It could've been one of the FBI agents in Mobile. It could've been one of the police officers in Destin or Sea Breeze. It could even have been his partner. "What do you want, Cantori?"

"Stay away from this case. I'm speaking as one friend to another. You've suffered enough."

"What are you talking about?" The fact that this man would still threaten him made him sick.

The low chuckle rolled over Ethan like an evil wave.

"I think you know exactly what I mean, Ethan. Watch your back. And keep a careful eye on those you love." His old enemy hung up the phone.

Ethan stared at it in his hand. Then stuffed it in his back pocket.

He needed to find his brother downstairs. And he needed to find his son. Had he put Charlie in danger again by following up on this?

But what was his other choice? *Not* following through?

His fingers curled into a fist. Barely, he resisted punching it through the wall.

He needed to find Tyler ASAP, and he had a good idea that his brother could be found in the kitchen. As he walked down the hall, he heard a noise from Kelsey's room. Babble, babble, babble. Silence. A little louder: babble, babble, babble. *Squeal.*

How was Kelsey sleeping through that?

As he went a little farther down the hall, he glanced into an open door. Kelsey lay curled in the corner of a sofa in a small sitting room, still in the clothes she'd worn the night before. She was sound asleep, her arm flung out beside her.

She was cute. Her dark hair curled almost to her waist. She wore casual sweatpants and a T-shirt that had a picture of Africa holding up two fingers like a peace sign. He was pretty sure he'd seen a celebrity wearing that on the cover of a magazine. Definition of an oxymoron?

Janie squealed again. Kelsey rolled onto her side

and tucked her fist under her cheek. She wouldn't sleep through that noise for long.

Gracie seemed to have blankets lying around everywhere. He pulled a rust-colored one from the end of the couch to cover Kelsey up. As he did, he saw the bottoms of her feet were bloodied and bruised.

His jaw tightened. She'd been running full out last night. Running from people shooting at her. And she hadn't once stopped to think about herself, only Janie—putting herself between the baby and danger. She was going to pay the price for that today. He dropped the blanket over her shoulders and stepped away, shaking his fingers to avoid clenching that fist again.

Anger management skills. He apparently needed some.

The door from this sitting room connected to the guest room that they'd chosen for Kelsey. He eased it open. Big blue eyes blinked at him over the top rail of the crib. She squealed again and bounced, rocking the bed.

"Shh."

She tilted her head.

"Hey, Janie-girl." She smiled at him. "Don't you remember the doctor said you're not supposed to get too excited?"

Ethan wasn't sure the doctor would believe it if they told him about escaping from gunmen and a late-night run across the bay. As he got closer, Janie looked up at him and raised her arms. There was such confidence in those eyes, and for just a second, he wanted to say, *Don't trust me.*

She was cute in her little flowered sleeper, and probably wet, if he remembered babies in the morning. Also, probably hungry. Hungry he could handle.

He picked her up from the crib and as he brought her closer, he got a whiff of the most noxious fumes. Was it… Oh, no. It most definitely was.

Ethan started back toward the sitting room and Kelsey. After all, Kelsey was the one who had official custody of the imp currently grinning at him from her perch on his arm. Dirty diapers would definitely be the purview of the official foster parent.

But then he remembered her feet and how exhausted she must've been to fall asleep on the couch like that. He sighed. "Okay, girl. Looks like it's just you and me. You're going to have to bear with me."

He laid her on the bed and looked around for a diaper. The bag was on the dresser at least ten feet away. He muttered under his breath. "Really? The bag has to be way over there?"

He may not have been a dad for long, but even he knew not to leave a baby Janie's age on the bed. He picked her back up to get the bag. He was exhausted and he hadn't even started the real work yet.

When he laid her back on the bed, she had a look on her face as if she were laughing at some private joke that only she knew. "Yeah, yeah, I know. I'm out of practice. Now where are those wipes?"

He unzipped her and nearly gagged. "What kind of crime scene do we have here, little miss? I think we might need the hazmat team."

Ethan undid the tabs on the diaper and, holding his

breath, cleaned her up as fast as he could. He turned to reach for the dry diaper and nearly lost her as she crawled like lightning toward the edge of the bed. "Whoa there, girl. You can't go anywhere without your drawers on."

He got the diaper on with no further drama and stuck her feet back in the footy holes. She tried to crawl out a couple of times, but he distracted her with his cell phone long enough to get her zipped back up and give his hands a quick swipe with one of her baby wipes.

She was ready to go.

He, on the other hand, was pouring sweat. Wrangling a toddler was a workout. "All right, peanut, you're ready to roll. Want to go downstairs and see what the master chef is cooking for breakfast?"

She bounced again, which he figured was as close to a yes as he was going to get. He walked her downstairs and into the kitchen, where it looked like a small nuclear device had exploded. "Whoa. What happened here?"

Pots were thrown haphazardly into the sink, and flour residue was scattered over every surface in the kitchen. Ethan was pretty sure there was a squirt of maple syrup on the wall.

"I was a little thrown off my game by some middle-of-the-night arrivals and the fact that my wife got called out this morning." His brother, in a cook's smock and baseball cap, shot him a look.

"Anything I can do to help?"

Tyler plated a stack of fluffy pancakes, sprinkled it with a flourish of powdered sugar and garnished it with a fan of sliced strawberry as a teenager with a perky red ponytail came flying through the door to the dining room.

"Pancakes." Tyler slid them across the work surface to her as she picked up a fresh pot of coffee.

"Oh, you're good, Mr. Clark." She backed out of the room. "This is the last one."

"I know." Tyler leaned against the counter, grabbed a bottle of water and swigged. "Now, what can I do for you?"

"Got a pancake for the little lady?"

Tyler grinned, chucked Janie under the chin and handed her a triangle of toast, which she immediately began to chew on. "I think that can be arranged. And for you?"

"The same would be good." Ethan hitched Janie up on his hip and ignored the toast crumbs littering his borrowed shirt as Tyler cracked eggs into a ceramic bowl. "I know we're trouble, but I need to—"

Tyler stopped midcrack on the fourth egg and turned to give Ethan a hard stare. "You're kidding me, right? I've barely seen you since you moved back here. I'm glad you felt like you could come to me for help."

The teenager came back through the dining room door, breaking up the moment and Ethan's opportunity to talk to his brother. She had a short, wooden high chair under one arm and the coffeepot in the other hand. "Figured you could use this. And we need more coffee. Those special ops types can put away some caffeine."

"No kidding. Coffee coming up. In the meantime,

grab another pitcher of orange juice out of the fridge, and there's at least one more basket of muffins in the warmer." Tyler grabbed the whisk from the counter and began to whip the eggs into a frothy mixture.

Ethan poked Janie's legs through the holes in the high chair and shoved her closer to the kitchen island. She picked a wooden spoon up from the counter and banged it.

"We might have mutiny here if those pancakes take much longer. Don't you have some Cheerios or something?"

Janie squealed again.

Tyler laughed. "Upper cabinet, left-hand side. I think there's some left from the last time the human vacuum visited."

Ethan pulled a yellow box out of the cabinet. "By human vacuum, I assume you mean Marcus?"

"Did we eat that much when we were fourteen?" Tyler dipped pancake batter onto the griddle.

Ethan laid a few round pieces of cereal on the counter in front of Janie. "Oh, yeah, we definitely did. Don't you remember Mom complaining about how she was going to have to get a second job so she could pay the grocery bill?"

He looked up, wondering how he was going to manage a smile for his brother's benefit, but Tyler was pouring beans into a fancy coffeepot.

He flipped the pancakes then turned around, twirling the spatula and snagging it out of the air with another laugh. "Right. And then she decided to do it all over again with Marcus. Mom's a saint."

"Yeah, she is." The voice came from the back door. Gracie walked in, snatched the spatula from her husband and smacked him with it. He grabbed her around the waist and laid a kiss on her that made Ethan want to turn away, give them a minute of privacy.

He noted her black cargo pants, combat boots and T-shirt that said CRT in large letters on the front. "Did the Crisis Response Team have a call-out this morning?"

"Yes." Gracie smiled. "It wasn't a big deal. A grocery store manager called because of a suspicious bag. Turned out to be a diaper bag slid halfway under a shelf. We found it on video being dropped from the cart yesterday afternoon. Complete accident."

When Janie screeched, Ethan dropped a few more Cheerios onto the counter.

Tyler slid a pancake onto a plastic plate for Janie. Ethan opened drawers until he found a knife and began to cut it into small pieces while Tyler put the other three pancakes on a plate for him.

Gracie dusted the pancakes with powdered sugar and placed the plate in front of Janie, then turned to Ethan. "Hungry?"

"Unbelievably hungry." Janie gave a toothy smile as she fisted the first piece and shoved it in her mouth. "Are you sure you don't want these, Gracie? Tyler can make more."

"Tyler can make more," his brother mimicked. "Like it's just that easy."

Ethan and Gracie looked at each other and Gracie

burst out laughing. "It's okay, hotshot, you're off the hook. I ate at Sip This with the guys."

Janie raised her hands up for Ethan to pick her up. "Hang tight, girl, I'm not finished eating."

"I've got this." Tyler picked her up.

She screamed and reached for Ethan.

"Wow, she doesn't like you." Gracie walked over to her. "I'll get her. Come with Aunt Gracie."

The screaming dulled to a whimper with Gracie, but Janie leaned toward Ethan, motioning with her hands out. Gracie made a rueful face. "I think she wants you, Ethan."

"She knows me, that's all." He shoved the last bite of pancake into his mouth and took the baby from Gracie. "She has a heart condition so she can't get upset."

"Poor baby." Gracie tickled Janie's foot, making her grin through her tears.

"Is that my hostage negotiator I hear in the kitchen making a baby cry?" A man dressed in full tactical gear stepped into the room and glanced around.

In that second, Ethan's mind slowed into that weird time warp when every thought flies at hyperspeed, and yet other people's motions are slow, like stop-motion video. The man at the door was a cop, or former cop, and he'd known Ethan as a drug dealer, the sidekick of a confidential informant.

The guy's eyes flickered and went flat as he recognized Ethan, and less than a second later, he'd pulled a weapon.

In a move guaranteed to make any criminal quake, he leveled the gun at Ethan. "Don't move."

Gracie gaped. "Brad? What are you—"

Ethan cut her off, holding Janie out to her. "Gracie, take the baby upstairs to Kelsey. She's going to cry again and she can't get overexcited, so get her to Kelsey as fast as you can."

As Gracie took the baby, Ethan raised his hands away from his body.

Tyler turned around from the griddle. "Ethan, you sound so ser— Whoa! Brad, meet my brother, Ethan. I don't know who you think you're pointing that Glock at, but I assure you, he's not who you think he is."

Brad flicked his eyes to Tyler and back to Ethan again, but didn't lower the gun. "Brothers?"

"As in the kind where we share a biological mother." The note of laughter in Tyler's voice was unmistakable, just as the hint of steel was.

"Brad's my guest here," he said to Ethan. Which Ethan knew was also designed to get Brad to mind his manners.

Ethan slowly lowered his hands. "Brad, you knew me as Connor Praytor. I was undercover with Raymond Jenks's crew in Mobile. The things that you saw me do were in that context. I was a Fed."

"Undercover?" Brad looked at Tyler for affirmation.

"He's former FBI. I think somebody had too much coffee this morning. You know, you have to be careful with that Ethiopian blend." Tyler walked between Ethan and Brad, nonchalantly putting himself in the line of fire. His voice turned cold as he spoke to Brad. "You should know that I wouldn't let anyone into Recovery

Cove who I didn't vet completely. Put your weapon away."

"Tyler, it's fine." Ethan didn't hear screaming, so he figured that Gracie had gotten Janie settled with Kelsey. He took four steps to the coffeepot and poured himself a cup, loose and easy, as if no one was holding a gun on him. "Three, almost four years ago, I was undercover with Jenks for five months."

He turned back to face Brad and took a sip of his coffee. "I can understand why you would be confused. And if you're here at Recovery Cove, then I can understand why you would be a little jumpy."

Brad holstered his weapon. "I wasn't confused and I'm not jumpy. Last time I saw you, you were a criminal."

"True." Ethan shrugged. He couldn't argue with that. "I don't work in Mobile anymore, and I don't work undercover anymore."

He saw the light dawn in Brad's eyes. "Oh, right. I remember when your—"

"Thanks for not shooting my brother in my kitchen, Brad." Tyler slid a plate of pancakes onto a tray and added a small pitcher of syrup. "Here, Ethan. Take these up to Kelsey. Tell her I'll send someone up with something to drink in a few minutes."

Ethan took the tray and climbed the stairs. Having a gun held on him was old business. A crying baby with a heart condition, not so much. The whole time, he'd been waffling between wondering if Brad was really going to shoot him and worrying that Janie was upstairs in some kind of crisis.

He guessed his priorities were in the right place.

FIVE

The knock at the door caught Kelsey just as she was easing her feet into the pan of warm water that Gracie had brought in. She hissed out a breath, her eyes tearing up as the water seeped into the cuts on the bottom of her feet. Her feet hurt so badly, she couldn't walk on them, not the way they were.

"I got it." Gracie opened the door and Ethan walked in with a tray of food.

He raised his eyebrows at the water. She made a face. "I didn't even notice last night that they were hurting. Adrenaline, I guess."

"Some of Tyler's pancakes ought to make you feel better." He slid the tray onto her lap and smiled as Janie crawled on all fours to the couch, where she pulled up to investigate. "Hey, peanut, you already had breakfast. Let Kelsey have hers."

"Ma-Ma."

Ethan's eyes shot to hers. "Did you hear that?"

"She definitely said Mama." Gracie rolled a ball toward Janie, who got momentarily distracted and sat down again. "She's really getting attached to you."

Kelsey stopped with the fork halfway to her mouth. "She probably didn't know what she was saying. *Mama* is one of the first words that babies say."

Janie threw the ball and it rolled about halfway back to Gracie. Gracie smiled. "You're right, but either way, I think it's a good thing that she's able to attach. It means that she's been loved. She understands it on the most basic level, at least."

Kelsey's insides felt ragged, like the bottoms of her feet. She was already attached, too, and she should have known better. "Thanks. I guess I needed to hear that. I don't want to hurt her more when she has to leave me."

Janie pulled up on the sofa again, but before she could get to a standing position, she plopped back down on the ground. Her lips primped up and she started to cry. Ethan picked her up, nuzzling her cheek. "Hey now, what are you making a fuss about?"

Gracie gave Ethan a pointed look. "What about work?"

"I've got a couple of days off in a row starting today, but I'll call and schedule a couple more. What about you, Kelsey? Did you call your office to let them know what was going on?"

"Yes. I told my boss that I needed some personal time for a few days to deal with the baby's health issues. It really puts them at a disadvantage to be a person down. I feel guilty." Kelsey put her fork down, her eyes on Janie, who was patting Ethan on the chest. "It's true that she needs special care, especially now. And she's really cute."

Gracie stood, patting the pockets of her cargo pants. "She's adorable. Less adorable, but still needy, is the team of police commandos downstairs that I'm supposed to teach hostage negotiation. I better get moving."

"Sorry about Brad," Ethan said to Gracie. Janie laid her head on his shoulder and then popped it back up to see if he was watching. He patted her on the back as he added, "I didn't have any idea there would be someone I knew in this group."

Man, he looked good holding that baby, and he was opening up more every day, thanks to the toddler in his arms. Kelsey didn't want to think what would've happened to them if he hadn't been there last night.

Gracie paused in the door. "Don't worry about it. It's fine. Brad needs to dial it back a few notches. He's the team leader. It was his request to do team building along with R&R. Personally, I think they needed the R&R more after a rough year. I'm out for a while, but call down if you need anything."

Gracie left and Ethan eased to a sitting position beside her, letting Janie slide to the floor to play with the toys Gracie had brought in.

He picked up the towel and first-aid kit that Gracie had left beside the pan of water. "You ready to get your feet out of there?"

"I can manage."

"I'm sure you can, but it will be easier if I help." He opened the towel.

She stared at it for a second. It had been a long time

since someone took care of her. She laid first one foot and then the other in it.

He patted her feet gently with the towel. Tears came to her eyes, a lump growing in her throat. Not because it hurt. It did, but the pain came from a completely different place. When her mom and dad died, she'd been adopted by another missionary family. They'd been loving parents, but it wasn't the same. She was ten, and at that age in the mission field, she'd been expected to pull her own weight.

It had been years since anyone had touched her with tenderness, with a touch that was meant to care for her alone. She loved her adopted family, had a slew of adopted brothers and sisters, but there had been no one to dry her tears when she skinned a knee. Or hold her in the night when she was lonely and afraid.

"Are you okay?" Ethan's voice was soft, the smooth, easy quality roughened by a night of little sleep.

"Yeah, just thinking. I'm fine." She smiled at him and pushed aside the thoughts, automatically reaching for the toy that Janie handed her. "What was the deal with that guy downstairs?"

He hesitated.

She prodded, "Gracie just said he was a hothead and you didn't want him to scare Janie."

"He mistook me for someone else. Someone he knew from the past."

She nodded, the lump in her throat back as Janie held her arms out to be picked up and Ethan began to dab antibiotic ointment on her cuts.

He shook his head. "It just made me more aware

that my past, my work with the Bureau, all ties into this somehow. There are people out there who wouldn't hesitate to kill me. Or you, if you got in the way."

Kelsey drew in a breath. It wasn't fair for him to shoulder the blame. "You're not the bad guy here. The people who did this to you and to these children, those are the bad guys, not you."

He looked down at her feet, holding them in his hands, the gesture strangely intimate. "Maybe, but if I hadn't been working undercover, Amy and Charlie wouldn't have been targets. There's no way to undo that."

She knew too well the pain of trying to undo the past, of what-iffing everything. If her parents hadn't been in Rwanda, if her village hadn't been on that particular highway, if…if…if.

"I know how you feel." At his sharp look, she said, "I do, Ethan. But all the what-ifs in the world can't undo what happened. The only thing you can do is move forward and live your life in a way that would make them proud."

Ethan turned aside, reaching for a bandage, and for a second she thought she'd made a big mistake. But she didn't know how to be any other way than straightforward.

He looked back, nodding slowly. "This case has dredged up feelings I didn't remember I had. For two years I've been like a dead man walking. But I don't think—I know—Amy wouldn't want that. She was too full of life for that."

"She sounds like a special person."

He nodded again. "It's hard to believe it's been two years." He looked up then. "I promise I'm going to do everything I can to find my son, and then I'm going to do everything I can to make sure his life is as safe and happy as it can be."

"I think your wife would be proud of the man you are, Ethan."

He stared at her toes, and the purple, sparkly toenail polish seemed a little foolish now. Of course, it had been picked by an eleven-year-old, a foster child who had won a trip to the nail salon with her by getting all As last quarter. Finally, he said, "I'm working on it."

Janie threw herself across Kelsey's feet into Ethan's lap.

Kelsey smiled, even though the lump in her throat just kept getting bigger. Regardless of whatever else was going on, there were young children whose lives were forever going to be altered by the outcome of this investigation. "If we can't leave here, how are we going to find out who Janie is? Besides the obvious need to find out her identity, it's really the only lead we have to find Charlie."

"I made a call last night. There's a guy Tyler's worked with before. He's a whiz at technology. If there's anything to be found, Nolan can find it. And he'll be here this afternoon." Ethan pulled the paper tabs off the last plastic bandage and taped it into place on the sole of her foot.

His hands were still on her feet, making it hard for her to think about anything else but the contact. She stared at them. When he didn't speak again, she slowly raised her eyes. They locked with his.

In the morning light, his eyes were so blue, so sincere.

"Thank you. It's been a while since anyone's tended a boo-boo for me." She grinned.

"You deserve someone to take care of you. You work hard." He gathered the paper and tube of ointment and tucked them all into the box.

She reached in her pocket for her cherry ChapStick and searched her mind for a change of subject, away from her and what she deserved or didn't deserve. "So where is Nolan coming in from?"

"Not sure. Not sure anyone knows, actually. He's pretty private. But he's the best and if he comes up with a lead, I'll follow up on it."

She started to protest, but remembered the sleepy baby in her arms. Someone had to be Janie's protector from right here. Last time she checked, she'd been the one elected. It was her job. It was also her passion. She wasn't going to let any child be alone in the world without someone to stand with them, for them.

A tap came from the doorway. She looked up to see Ethan's brother. He held a tray with a couple of pots and some mugs. "I wasn't sure if you'd like coffee or tea."

"Tea."

"Coffee."

She and Ethan spoke at the same time.

Tyler laughed and slid the tray onto a side table.

"Luckily I brought both. And a fresh cup of milk for the little lady."

"Milk." Janie perked up.

"Another word. Either she's picking them up really quickly, or the stress she felt at changing environments and caregivers is easing enough for her to start talking." Kelsey took the sippy cup from Tyler and held it out for Janie.

"I'll take her while you drink your tea." Ethan took Janie and settled her on his lap. She leaned against his chest and bounced her feet, sipping out of her cup.

Kelsey's eyes were stinging again. She must be more tired than she thought. Or it could be that the sight of the big lawman taking such gentle care of Janie made her heart ache. "I need to get the medication that the doctors prescribed for her to keep her heart rate stable. Be right back."

"Your feet—" Ethan started to get up, but Kelsey hobbled away, disappearing through the door into the bedroom.

"She might be stubborn enough to handle you." His brother Tyler kicked back in his chair with a superior look on his face.

"Now look, just because you're all cozy and happy with Gracie doesn't mean you have to start in on me." Ethan caught Janie's eyes drooping. Evidently, she did, too, because her little head popped up and she slid off his lap onto the floor.

"I'm not starting in on you, just joking around. You can be a little testy." Tyler poured a cup of coffee and handed it to Ethan. "This might help. Though you might want to reconsider the caffeine."

"I've been held at gunpoint twice in two days, shot at one of those times. Forgive me for being a little 'testy.'" He glanced at his brother. He knew Tyler was teasing but the jabs hit a little close to home. Kelsey was the first person Ethan had gotten close to in a long time, but there was a reason for that. He wasn't looking for love. How could he be?

"Ethan, in all seriousness, why are you doing this? I understand helping her escape last night. I'm all for helping out people in need or obviously we wouldn't have Restoration Cove, but it seems like—"

"You think I feel like this is my shot at redemption for losing Charlie and Amy."

"Do you?"

Ethan stood and stuck his hand in his pocket, noting Janie's guarded expression as he did. He pulled out the picture of Charlie that he'd printed after he found all the baby pictures and tossed it into Tyler's lap.

His brother picked it up and studied it. "I don't understand. What is this?"

"It's a picture taken of Charlie two weeks after the night he supposedly died."

"Supposedly…"

"Yes. He was kidnapped, Tyler."

His brother stared at the photo. "I don't even know what to say to this. You're sure?"

"As sure as I can be without seeing him face-to-face. I don't know how, but this little baby is my connection to finding him." Ethan stared at the picture for a moment. "And if I had any doubts, they disappeared when I got a call this morning from one of the men I was investigating for human trafficking. Tyler, I haven't heard the slightest thing about this case until Janie, and now suddenly I'm getting a call from Tony Cantori?"

"I don't know what to say." Tyler studied Janie as she played quietly on the floor. "I can't even process this."

Ethan stared out the window toward the blue water of the bay. "Believe me, I know. I found Charlie's photo in with a file of hundreds of pictures of other children. There is something much larger going on than kidnapping the child of one FBI agent for revenge." He held Janie's cup out to her as she crawled to him and pulled up on the edge of the sofa.

"Clearly there's a lot that we don't know." Tyler stood and paced to the edge of the room, and Janie went still on the floor, watching him.

Ethan picked her up. "I think Janie was held somewhere until someone left her for me to find, knowing that I would take care of her because I would do anything in my power to find my son."

"And finding Charlie does what? Takes down the operation? Saves other children from the same fate?"

Ethan shrugged. "Maybe. I don't see myself as some savior. I just want my son back."

"You certainly saved one little girl." Kelsey's voice from the door startled Ethan. "She adores you."

He looked down at Janie. When he first found her, he had seen her as someone to rescue. And yeah, he had to admit, there was a small part of him that had seen his son in her—that thought if his son had been alone and in need, he would want someone to help.

Slowly, though, he was coming to know Janie's little personality. He knew he would do anything for the little angel playing on the floor beside him, a fact that scared him to death. Because he knew that love made a man more vulnerable—and he didn't ever want to be that vulnerable again.

Kelsey limped back into the room on the side of one foot and the heel of the other and sank to the floor where Janie played, squirting a prefilled syringe into her mouth before the baby could even protest.

"Impressive," Tyler noted. He dug around in his back pocket and pulled out a cell phone, handing it to Kelsey. "I forgot to give you this earlier. I hope you don't mind, but we had your old number forwarded to this phone, since you lost yours."

"Wouldn't someone be able to trace her to this location?" Ethan voice was tight with concern.

"Thank you for asking, Granny Worry." Tyler looked at Kelsey. "The new phone is secure just like yours, so even if someone calls your old number and tries to locate you, they won't be able to. It's really important that you don't tell anyone where you're staying, Kelsey. Even the people in your office."

She nodded. She knew that even her coworkers were not above suspicion, that anyone could be corrupted. But it was their job to keep children safe.

"It may seem extreme, but we keep a couple of these phones on hand. Obviously that we exist is no secret, but we want Restoration Cove to be a safe haven for those who come here."

The doorbell rang. Tyler stood. "It's probably Nolan. I'll go meet him. He'll want to set up in the library."

Ethan followed Tyler out the door into the hall.

"I'll be down in a bit. I want to meet Nolan, but I need to get Janie down for a nap." Her new phone rang, and for a moment, she just stared at it. Within seconds, both men had returned to the doorway.

She picked it up. It was probably just work. "Kelsey Rogers."

After listening a few seconds, she said, "Thanks for letting me know. Yes, you can fax the medical file to…" She looked at Tyler, the question on her face.

Tyler supplied the number for their secure fax line and Kelsey repeated it into the phone. "Definitely keep me posted on your findings."

She hung up the phone and turned to Ethan. "The warrant came through for Janie's medical records. The doctor faxed them to my office. We're going to send an officer to the address they show for Janie and ask some questions. They'll call us with any new information."

On the floor, Janie couldn't get a block into a bucket and dissolved into tears. Ethan picked her up again. "I could try to get her to sleep if you want to wait on the call."

"No, go talk to Nolan. Get the file. I'll meet you downstairs in a few minutes." She held her arms out to Janie and the baby lurched into them, immediately laying her head on Kelsey's shoulder.

"Tyler will make sure the papers get through, and

we'll start Nolan working on connections to the address in the file." Ethan patted Janie on the back, his face serious. "We're going to get to the bottom of this, don't worry."

He made Kelsey feel safe. He made her feel like someone cared. Special moments she'd missed when she lost her parents—those were things she tried to provide for the foster children in her care.

Now someone was showing her the same care.

It meant more to her than she could've imagined. And she was going to have to let him go. Because even she knew he wasn't in this for a relationship. He was in it to find his son.

She was a means to an end because she held the baby that was the key to it all.

SIX

Ethan leaned over the fax machine as it spit out pages. "Come on."

He'd known his son was alive for approximately twenty-four hours, and the tension inside him was hitting the unbearable point. He needed information and he needed it now.

He picked up a page, glanced at it and shoved it in front of Nolan. "Here. Here's the address."

Nolan took the sheet and placed it to the side on the shiny surface of the cherrywood desk. "Dude. I don't even have the system hooked up yet."

"Sorry." Ethan stacked the pages of the medical file, taking a deep breath. He stabbed his fingers through his hair, giving him a bed-head look. "Can I help?"

The guy had been attached in some way or another to every agency Ethan could think of. His security clearance was probably higher than the president's. He shot Ethan a look. "No."

Ethan paced the room. "The address is in Jacksonville. Maybe that's where they moved their operation.

It would make sense with the tourism industry and the port."

"Not to mention the I-95 corridor." Nolan powered up the computer. "Okay, give me the address—and look through those papers. If those are medical records, you should have some other info. A copy of a driver's license, or a Social Security number—something."

His fingers flew on the keys. "So I have some databases that I normally check for information on property owners. If she gave the correct address, we might be able to find information on the owner or renter."

More tapping on the keyboard. He made a noise.

"What? What was that?" Ethan leaned forward.

Nolan shoved him back. "Don't hover. It's listed under a corporation name. Let me do some more digging. It's probably a shell, but I might be able to come up with something."

Kelsey appeared in the door. Ethan straightened. "Baby asleep?"

"Yes, but that's not why I'm here. I got a call from the cops in Maryland. There was nothing in the house. It had been cleaned out." She looked defeated, dark circles making her eyes look bruised. "Wait—did the fax come through? What's Janie's name?"

He picked up a page from the fax, turned it to show her. "Her name is Jane Peters."

"Peters? My guess is the real name is more like Petrovka, but they Americanized it. I wonder what her mother called her. Children in Russia always have nicknames, even if the name is longer than their real name."

She blew out a breath. "Will we ever be able to find out for sure?"

"Don't worry. We're not out of it yet." Ethan circled an arm around her waist, and she leaned into him, lifting one of her sore feet to rest it on the other one. "Everyone leaves traces. We just need someone who can find them."

"Luckily you have that person sitting right here." Nolan tapped on the keys. "Okay, I searched the name listed on the form. Viktoria Arsov didn't use her real Social Security number. There's even a note in the file that she forgot her driver's license when she was in the office with the baby. But we can cross-reference the name she gave with the address we have."

He hummed a little as he typed and scrolled. "Okay, she doesn't have a bank account, but she has a credit card in the same name with a slightly different spelling, using that address."

Kelsey shifted her weight to the other foot, but they were both so sore that it didn't really help. "I can get a court order for the credit card records, but it might take a little while."

Nolan tapped the keys a few more times, and a paper came spewing out of the printer. "She used that card three hours ago, about forty-five minutes from here, at a hotel just outside Fort Walton Beach." He whipped the paper out of the tray and held it up.

Ethan snatched it. "I'm going."

Kelsey blocked the doorway. "Ethan, you have to call the sheriff's office or the SBPD for help. You have no idea what this woman is capable of or if she's even alone."

Tyler walked in, dropped into one of the leather reading chairs and hooked one foot over the other knee. "I have to agree with Kelsey on this one. There's nothing good that can come from going alone, but lots that can go wrong."

"This woman is the only lead I have to finding my son." He looked into Kelsey's eyes and took her hand. "I don't want to leave you, but you'll be safe here, I promise."

He let her hand drop as he strode away without giving them a chance to say more. He wasn't kidding. It was hard leaving her here. Harder still was knowing Charlie was out there somewhere and not knowing where. Or how to get to him.

"Ethan." The soft voice behind him stopped him in motion as he reached for the doorknob.

His shoulders dropped. "I'm sorry, Kels—I have to go. I have to take this chance."

"I understand. Just be careful, please. This is the person who left a baby defenseless in the middle of the ocean."

He gave her a quick smile, meant to reassure. "Janie's got you now. She's far from defenseless." He pushed open the back door. "Don't worry. I'll be back soon. Hopefully with the woman who knows the details of Janie's life."

Kelsey pressed something into his hand. "We'll have backup meet you there. Your brother said to give you these."

The same

fear

hope

Keys. He wouldn't have gotten very far without them, evidence that he wasn't thinking as clearly as he should be—guess he needed the backup they were sending after all. "Thanks." He touched her cheek. "You won't even know I'm gone."

He walked away.

His baby had been taken from him. He could barely breathe at the thought that Charlie might be alive. For so long there hadn't been a whisper of hope in his life. There had been nothing to look forward to. He'd been an empty shell.

Hope hurt.

But he was ready for it. Charlie needed him. And he needed Charlie, to know that he was okay. To know that his little boy hadn't suffered—wasn't suffering the way Ethan had these last two years.

He glanced back at the house and saw Kelsey framed in the doorway to the kitchen. The early afternoon sunlight shone on her face, gilding her in its light. She was tough and sweet, had to be to hang in there in the job she did. He had amazing respect for her.

Truthfully, she was beginning to mean something to him in a way that was completely unexpected. He didn't know what to do with the knowledge, or even what it meant, but there it was.

And that kind of hope hurt, too. He felt like he was coming apart at the cracks. Every bit of sticking together that he'd done in the last two years seemed to be shredding in the face of these new developments.

The only thing he knew to do was stay busy, chase

down the leads to find his son and baby Janie's past and do everything in his power to keep both of them safe.

He could think about the rest later.

Kelsey watched Ethan drive away and fought the urge to, in a fit of temper, hold her breath until he returned. She had a little baby upstairs depending on her, depending on both of them, to find out what in the world was going on.

She limped back into the library. Ethan and Tyler's friend, Nolan, had his head bent over the computer. He was talking to himself and typing. His hair was sticking up in all directions. He wore a tiny silver cross on leather threads around his neck. She hated to interrupt his work, but he was probably the only person who could help her. "Nolan?"

He didn't look up.

"Hello?"

The computer expert stopped typing and looked up, squinting eyes the color of aged whisky at her. "Sorry, I'm not good with names. Do I know you?"

She eased into a seat across the table from him, relieved to take some of the pressure off her feet. "I'm Kelsey, Ethan's friend."

"The social worker."

"Right, the social worker." As a general rule, she wasn't a fan of labels, but if it worked for him, she could deal. "I need some help. We found an SD card with photographs of infants that we believe were trafficked through illegal adoptions. I need to try to find these babies."

"You have photographs?" He reached into his bag and pulled out another laptop.

"I was thinking maybe there would be a way to search for pictures of those babies that were posted somewhere? I know we might not find all of them, but if we found some of them and could find the adoption states, I could subpoena the records, which might bring out more information."

"Yeah, it could be a good start at tracking down the people who would actually sell a child to a person desperate enough to buy one." The anger in his voice took her aback.

He blinked and the anger disappeared. "Sorry. It makes me a little upset that there are more than four hundred million orphans in the world, but babies are being trafficked for profit."

It was the first sign of emotion that she'd seen from the very efficient, methodical Nolan. Also preoccupied, disheveled and disorderly and, apparently, passionate about some things. Intriguing.

"I understand. I was adopted at the age of ten. If my parents hadn't taken me in, there's no telling where I would've ended up." She stuffed her hands into the pants of her borrowed jeans, the legs cuffed because Gracie was two inches taller. "So, is there a program like that?"

"Sit down." He slid a laptop across the table to her. "I have…access, we'll say, to a reverse image search. It's highly specialized. You enter the picture, the program searches the internet for images with similar reference points. You should have some luck, but it's going to take time. You'll have to enter each photo individually."

An hour later, she'd found four children out of the forty that she'd run through the search engine. She was surprised how many people blogged about their adoption journey.

So she had names to start with for the four, and those she was passing across the table to Nolan to start background searches. He was having better luck than she was at finding out real information.

She heard a noise and looked up, wondering if she should worry about the lighting fixtures above them. It sounded like someone knocking on a door, but she had a sneaking suspicion that it was a toddler, banging the side of her bed against the wall. "You'll have to excuse me. I think I'm needed upstairs."

"What? Oh." Nolan scrubbed a hand through his curly hair, making it stand up even more. "You can take the computer with you if you like. It's not like I can use both of them. If you find anything more, you can always bring it to me or shoot me an email. There's wireless here and it's safe to use."

Safe to use the wireless. Something else she wouldn't have considered. "Thanks, Nolan. You've been a lot of help."

Kelsey limped up the stairs as fast as she could, taking most of the weight on the handrail. She went through the sitting room to drop off the computer before opening the door to the blue-and-brown bedroom, an inexplicable joy filling her at the thought of the blue-eyed, towheaded tot on the other side. She peeked around the corner.

"Peep-eye, Janie."

Janie whipped her head around, a smile breaking on her face. She laughed.

Kelsey lifted the toddler out of the porta-crib. "You need a clean diaper ASAP, young lady."

She quickly changed Janie into a dry diaper and clean clothes, then lifted her into her arms. "There you go, munchkin, all done."

Janie moved her hands, almost like a referee signaling "safe," and repeated the gesture again. *All done.*

Safe

A few years back, Kelsey had taken a workshop on baby signing for continuing ed hours. She recognized the sign. How would this baby, who had been abandoned and barely spoke, know the sign? It didn't fit.

It was possible that it was a fluke and she didn't mean to do it. She put Janie on the bed again and touched her arm. "Janie, more milk?"

As she spoke she made the signs with her hands, putting the fingers of both hands together for *more* and making a squeezing motion with one hand for *milk*.

Janie immediately brought her hands together. *More.*

Wow. Definitely not a fluke. Kelsey blew out a breath and held her arms out to the toddler. "Come on, we'll go get you some milk and a snack."

Even young babies learn rudimentary communication. She'd been so sad that Janie had been separated from the people who could communicate in her language, even though she knew it wouldn't be long before she learned to compensate.

Janie rarely cried like a normal baby, and she didn't talk. But she signed, something that had been proven to help babies communicate their needs. It was so interesting to Kelsey. What was more interesting was that it pointed to a mother who loved Janie enough to teach her.

A perplexing mystery.

"Hey, I figured your feet would be hurting. You hungry?" Gracie came in balancing a plate of cheese, crackers and grapes and two bottles of water. She had a sippy cup under her other arm. "Nolan told me the baby woke up."

"So you're through with your gig as the hostage negotiator?" Kelsey handed Janie a set of plastic car keys, one of the toys she carried in her big tapestry bag.

Gracie walked through the open door into the sitting room and dropped easily to the floor, crossing her legs underneath her. "This time I was playing the hostage. Unfortunately, the hothead team leader decided to go for the tactical solution too early and the 'hostage' and the 'hostage taker' were both killed." She rolled her eyes. "Since I'm officially dead, I decided they could spend the afternoon alone."

"Well, we're glad to see you." Kelsey spoke through the open door to Gracie then turned to the baby. "Want some milk?"

Janie lunged into Kelsey's arms, making the sign for *milk* as Kelsey carried her into the sitting room. Kelsey looked at Gracie, raising an eyebrow. "Did you see that?"

"She made a sign. How in the world did you figure

that out?" Gracie held the milk cup for Janie to grasp in her little hands.

"Complete accident." Kelsey dropped to the floor, where the toys still remained from the morning's play session. "It's not extremely unusual for a baby to sign, but she's so quiet."

"Maybe Ethan will come back with information that can help us." Gracie handed Janie a cracker as she crawled toward the plate. "I know this isn't much lunch for a toddler. I'll have the cook make something for her."

"By 'the cook,' you mean Tyler?"

"Of course." Gracie smiled. "I sure didn't marry him for his good looks. It was the fluffy pancakes that did me in. That and the studly sense of honor the Clark men have."

"Ethan definitely has it." Kelsey made the sign for *more* to Janie, who repeated it back to her. *More.* "This case, the fact that he didn't know about Charlie…he won't admit it, but it's killing him."

Gracie's smile faded. "I know it has to be. I've worked with a lot of cops and agents over the years. It's a rare one that isn't affected personally in some way, but what happened to Ethan is beyond anything I've ever seen."

"I'm hoping that finding Charlie can give him some closure. It's not going to be easy."

"Nolan mentioned that you were doing an image search. Did you have any luck?" Gracie handed Janie another cracker and laughed as she crushed it, scattering crumbs all over the carpet.

Kelsey held her hand out to Janie, who put the crushed cracker in her hand. "Oh, thank you. So sweet." To Gracie, she said, "I've run an image search on twenty-eight of the photographs. So far, I've found four exact matches. One on Facebook and three on adoption blogs. They posted the pictures as their dream of having children come true. It's heartbreaking."

"Are you sure the adoptions weren't legal?"

"I'm not sure of anything at this point. The only one we know wasn't legal was Ethan's son, Charlie's. Signs point to illegal adoption, though, which is another thing that the witness Ethan is hunting will be able to confirm or deny."

"Did you run an image search on Charlie's photo?"

Slowly, she nodded. "It was running when I heard Janie awake up here."

"So it's probably finished." Gracie looked at the computer sitting on the sofa.

Kelsey looked, too. Jumping crickets were banging around in her stomach. "I should look?"

Gracie nodded. "It was a brilliant idea to match the photos."

Kelsey rubbed her finger across the mouse pad and brought up the page. It beeped and the results popped up. Her eyes met Gracie's wide blue ones.

Now she had to decide what she was going to tell Ethan when he got back.

SEVEN

Ethan tapped the front of his bullet-resistant vest and waited impatiently behind the cops who had met him at the small hotel on the outskirts of Sea Breeze. Detective Joe Sheehan had met him here at the hotel with a tactical team of men used to banging on doors—and going through them—without knowing what they would find on the other side.

He and Joe had talked to the manager on duty and found out which room had been rented to the credit card in question. Now, she just had to be there.

With a nod from Joe, the cop by the door knocked. When there was no answer, he waved the manager forward to use the master key on the lock. He swiped the key and, with a look to confirm that they were through with him, left in a hurry. The two cops in front opened the door and entered the room, shouting their identities as police officers.

Within a few moments they were motioning him in. "The room's clear, sir. She's not here."

"You've gotta be kidding me." He went into the hotel room. The bed had been slept in. Used towels were on the floor and there were fast-food bags in the trash can. Viktoria Arsov had definitely been here.

But where had she gone?

He opened the drawer. There were a few items of clothing, but nothing to identify where she might be heading if she didn't return. And if she came back to see cops crawling the property, he would bet she wouldn't come back to this room.

There was a jacket hanging in the closet. He searched the pockets and found a movie ticket stub. Maybe she was spending her free time at the theater, staying out of sight. But the question in his mind was: Why had she stayed in the area after ditching the baby? Why had she taken the risk?

There was white dust on the floor of the closet. He picked up Arsov's suitcase to move it out of the way and very nearly put his fist through the wall at what he saw. Someone had sawed an eighteen-inch-by-eighteen-inch square through the wall of the hotel room into the next room, just small enough to hide behind the suitcase.

Just large enough for a person to fit through.

If Arsov had seen them, she very easily could've escaped.

He stormed into the bathroom and picked up the trash can. Hair color: brunette. If the deputies outside thought they were looking for a blonde, like Arsov's DMV photos reflected, she might've slipped right past them. He ran for the door of the hotel room, the deputies giving him strange looks.

"Did anyone come out of the room next door?

Room 224? Anyone come out of this room?" He pointed at the door, shouting at the cops outside.

Finally one stepped forward, an officer who had been posted in the parking lot. "Yes, sir. A young woman came out with her boyfriend about five minutes ago."

"Where did they go?" Aware that his anger was showing, Ethan tried to dial it back but failed. "Anyone?"

"She left in her car." A young guy, one of the hotel guests who had apparently come out to see the hoopla, answered. "I came out of the hotel room with her, but I'm not her boyfriend. She told me that her ex-husband was trying to have her arrested for stealing a car that she bought."

The kid looked miserable. Ethan rubbed a hand across his mouth. "What else did she say?"

"That all she needed was a way to get away and I wouldn't get in trouble."

Ethan nodded, the anger at having lost the only lead to his son dwindling. It wasn't this kid's fault. "Okay, thanks. One of these detectives will get a statement from you."

He waved Joe Sheehan over and walked out of the parking lot to where his car was parked on the street. He banged his hands on the steering wheel.

Their best lead was in the wind. And that left them with exactly nothing.

Ethan got permission to enter the grounds at Restoration Cove, the gates sliding open in front of him.

When he pulled in the driveway, the first thing he saw was a blanket on the grass and Kelsey sitting cross-legged with the baby crawling around her. Kelsey's hair was looped up in a ponytail.

She also had on different clothes than she'd been wearing this morning—jeans, a graphic T, a cardigan. Then he realized that Janie was dressed like a Baby Gap model, too.

He chuckled as he walked toward her. "Let me guess. Gracie sent their teenage help shopping for your clothes."

"Are you saying that I don't always dress this cool?"

"Not at all. It's actually not that far off from how you normally dress."

She laughed. "I know. I would totally wear this. Gracie sent her back to town for more practical baby clothes, though. This little sweater Janie has on? It has to be professionally cleaned."

Ethan dropped to the blanket, lying back and crossing his hands behind his head as he looked at the crystal-blue sky. He didn't want to bring up what happened at the hotel, even though he knew Kelsey would be curious. So he stalled. "I love fall in Florida. It gives you hope that the rest of the year isn't going to be as miserable as the summer."

Janie launched herself across the blanket and landed half on top of Ethan's chest. She patted his face.

"What happened, Ethan?" Kelsey's voice was quiet.

"She ran. Got out right under our noses." He shrugged

one shoulder, then rolled to face her, balancing his head on his hand, tickling Janie with the other one.

Janie flopped to her back, kicking her feet, grabbing Ethan's hand with both of her smaller ones. She was so cute, her joy innocent and infectious. He wanted to hold her close and protect her from anything bad that might come her way.

"Is she okay to play like this? I know she's not supposed to get too excited."

"I think she's fine." Kelsey touched his shoulder. "I'm sorry about the witness. Is there anything we can do?"

"Pray that she gets sloppy and uses her credit card again." He watched as Janie scooted closer to the edge of the blanket and touched the grass with her foot. She looked back to see if Kelsey was watching. "Viktoria Arsov is my only known connection to Charlie. I don't know how to find him without her, Kels."

"That's not going to be a problem." She went quiet for a couple seconds. "I know where he is."

He felt the pain in his gut, like he'd been sucker-punched. "What?"

"Nolan and I did an image search. I wasn't sure if it would work or if I should, but…they actually only live a couple of hours from here."

"They…" His voice was shaky. He steadied it and continued. "Kelsey, I need to know."

"I know. Let's go inside and I'll show you." She winced as she put the weight on her feet and reached for the baby.

"I'll get her. Even twenty extra pounds is too much

for those feet." He lifted Janie easily and settled her on his arm. She rubbed her cheek with her fingers.

"I think that might be her sign for *blankie*. She's really very communicative. Now that I've figured out that she knows signs, I'm starting to pick up more and more." Kelsey handed the tattered square of dingy pink to Janie, who immediately rubbed it against her cheek.

Ethan started for the house, took one look at the dinner preparation going on in the kitchen through the window and veered for the patio door off the living room. He could feel his heart pounding in his chest.

One way or another, the next few minutes would change his life.

Kelsey followed Ethan into the house, moving more slowly, her sore feet slowing her down. She and Nolan had talked about whether to even tell Ethan that she had found evidence of his son's whereabouts. In Nolan's black-and-white, binary world, he believed that telling Ethan would only make it harder on him.

It would, there was no question, because he wouldn't be able to go to his son, not now. Not without endangering Charlie further. He would need to provide protection for him, though. This investigation would put Charlie at risk, something she was sure Ethan had already thought of.

Ethan had been grieving the loss of his wife and son for two years. Maybe it was cruel to give him the information when he couldn't act on it, but in her opinion, it would be more cruel to keep the only information they had on Charlie from his biological father.

He held the door open for her, tension evident in the taut lines of his body. As tightly reined as she knew he held his emotions, she couldn't imagine the crazy ride he'd been on the last few days.

In the library, Nolan still sat over the keyboard, a bevy of empty root beer bottles on a separate table beside him.

"Nolan." Ethan knocked on the doorframe. "Kelsey said you found something."

"Actually, Kelsey found it. I only gave her the software. It's pretty cool. See, it works with photographs, analyzing about a thousand points of reference and then searching for—" He looked up at Ethan's face, his voice trailing off. "Get to the point?"

"That would be good."

Kelsey put her hand on Ethan's back. He was nearly vibrating with tension. Janie squirmed in his arms.

He handed the baby to Kelsey. "Please, Nolan."

Nolan's fingers flew on the keys. "One second. Let me just save this and…there."

The blog popped up. Called "And Then There Were Three," it was cute, decorated on the sides like a scrapbook with multicolored 3s, ribbons and photos. Ethan sucked in a breath at the photograph of a two, almost three-year-old boy wearing a cowboy hat—a little boy who had Ethan's unmistakable blue eyes.

Ethan leaned forward, making an unconscious sound.

Nolan stood and gave Ethan his seat. "Read it, dude. It's the story of their life from before they adopted their—" His eyes shot to Kelsey. "I mean, *your* kid. I'm, um, just going to go get something from somewhere. Else. Somewhere else."

He grabbed an armload of empty bottles and bolted from the room.

"You scare him, you know."

"He needs to get out more." Ethan didn't look up. He was staring at the computer screen, but hadn't moved it forward to read the entries.

"If you look at the side, you'll see the archives. You can start at the beginning. That's where she introduces herself and you'll see the original picture I found."

He moved the cursor over to the first entry. It hovered there for a long moment. Very deliberately, he clicked it. When it loaded he started reading.

Kelsey could see only his profile, but the muscles in his jaw worked as he read the story of the adoption. She'd had unabashed tears streaming down her face earlier. Even Nolan had cleared his throat a time or two, reading it.

Ethan was silent, his only movement his finger on the keyboard.

She ached to reach out to him, but didn't know how. Grieving for a child you believed gone from you forever, that was one thing. Finding that another family has had the joy of raising him—the same joy that was taken from you—there was no precedent for that.

She prayed silently for Ethan, that he could come to grips, somehow, with everything that had happened. He needed peace in the midst of the storm. If he didn't have it, he might not survive. And Kelsey knew that the Lord was the only source of that peace.

Janie fussed in her arms, and Kelsey eased toward the door.

"You don't have to go." He didn't look up from the computer, but his words stopped her.

Were they a plea for her to stay? The baby squirmed again, pushing away from her. Nolan appeared in the door, holding out his arms for Janie. She didn't know what to do. Up to this point, Janie had been pretty particular about who she would go to.

Nolan reached a little closer, and Janie leaned forward to grab a handful of his hair. He shot a grin at Kelsey and looped an arm around Janie's waist, hitching her high on his forearm. "Here we go. No problem, Uncle Nolan's got you."

She watched the computer whiz leave with the baby, some kind of protective mother instinct whispering that Janie would be safe with Nolan.

Ethan's shoulders were straight. He still hadn't moved, but as she returned to stand beside him, he took a shuddering breath. "She tried to get pregnant for years. Seven miscarriages. They chose Charlie because he was older, because the adoption agency told them he could be adopted right away. He was the answer to their prayers. Literally."

He turned to her, the gut-wrenching anguish he felt evident on his face. "I hadn't even thought about them. I'm so selfish that other than praying that Charlie was safe and happy, the people who adopted him never entered my mind. This is going to tear them apart at the seams. Who would know that better than I would?"

Ethan let his head drop to the back of the tall leather chair. He tried to define the emotions coursing through him, even as he worried that they were so big, they would swamp him. Jubilation that his son was alive, that he knew where he was, that he'd been adopted by a couple who obviously loved him.

Equally, as he clicked through the pages of this woman's blog—looking at pictures of Charlie as he got his teeth, as he took his first steps, as he went from a bottle to a cup—he realized there was such regret. An overwhelming sadness that the moments which were supposed to have been shared with Amy—those moments with Charlie had been shared by another couple.

"Looking at these photos…" He pressed his lips together as his voice broke and tried again. "I missed… so much."

Tears fell and he swiped at his face with one hand. With the other, he clicked on a photo of Charlie with his mouth open wide in a laugh. "He's beautiful."

"He looks like you. I knew we'd found him as soon as I saw him." Kelsey's hand was soft on his arm.

"How will they give him up? They love him so much. But I can't let him go again." He turned to her, his lashes black with dampness. He lifted one shoulder, let it drop. "I wouldn't survive it."

He pushed away from the table, walked to the window, the stir of emotions too much to contain. "What have I done?"

"This was not your fault, Ethan. You didn't cause this." She followed him to the window and put her arms around him, laying her cheek against his back. He let out his breath in a rush and just let himself be held.

He hadn't realized how much he'd missed it. How much he missed the comfort of another's touch. He turned to face her, pulling her into his arms. Her head fit right into the crook of his neck. He sucked in an uneven breath.

And realized in some way his own prayers had been answered. That no matter what he might feel sometimes, he wasn't going through this alone.

Kelsey turned her face to his. "I can't even believe this is actually happening. Two days ago, you and I were both having a perfectly normal day."

"And then we met Janie." He let the smile turn up the corner of his mouth. It felt good, with so much sadness, for there to be something to smile about.

"And then we met Janie," she repeated, as she reached a hand up to rub the shadow of a beard at his jawline. "It's going to be okay. We'll figure it out. We have to—there's no other choice."

"I want to storm those people's house and go into that cute little airplane room and take my son home with me." At the alarmed look on Kelsey's face, he quickly stopped himself with the truth. "I know I can't—I can't do it to them and I can't do it to Charlie. They're the only family he knows. They're his parents, not me."

His voice broke again as he said the last. But he was over pretending that he was okay, with any of this. He wasn't okay. He wouldn't be until this case was over. Until they figured out what happened to every baby in that file.

"Do you think the FBI is using similar software to this to search out these families?" Kelsey's thoughts were obviously on a similar track to his.

"Probably. Those photos are the only evidence we have that the adoption scam even happened, and the children the only connection to the crime that we have. Although, I guarantee you someone is trying to find the woman we looked for today. I can also guarantee you we're trying harder."

A squeal came from the living room. Kelsey's eyes locked with his. "I'll go."

He stopped her with his hand. "You've had her all day. I don't mind."

"We can both go."

Kelsey rounded the corner to the living room first and then stepped back quickly into the hall. "Look."

Ethan stepped in front of her and peered around the corner. Nolan was sitting on the couch with his legs stretched out lengthwise. Janie sat across his lap with an iPad on her lap.

"Okay, your turn. Tickle, tickle, tickle, Elmo." Nolan said it in a high-pitched voice. Kelsey slapped both hands over her mouth to keep the laugh from escaping.

Janie pressed the screen with her finger, and Elmo laughed. Janie squealed again, kicking her feet.

Ethan chuckled, too. Despite everything, she cracked him up. "She's really so cute."

"Isn't she, though?" Kelsey walked into the room and spoke up. "Hey there, pumpkin, whatcha doing?"

"Kids love technology." Nolan flipped his legs around and rearranged Janie to sit next to him on the couch. He looked tentatively at Ethan still leaning against the door to the living room. "Everything all right?"

Ethan didn't move. He also didn't lie. "No. But it is what it is. We'll get through it."

Ethan's brother walked into the room, drying his hands on the apron wrapped around his waist, the expression on his face serious. "Someone just pulled up to the gate. She says her name is Viktoria. She's looking for Ethan Clark."

"What? How did she find us?"

"My guess is she put a GPS tracker either in the baby's bag or somewhere on your car when she got away this morning." Tyler reached around his back to untie the apron.

Nolan stood and handed the baby off to Kelsey. "You're right in the middle of dinner prep for twelve people. Let me just grab my shoes from the other room." To Kelsey, he said, "Keep the iPad for now. I downloaded a couple of those 'make your baby a genius' videos."

Ethan knew that Nolan was the best at what he did. He could find anyone anywhere, break any code, set up the best security system, but as backup went...

Tyler must've noted his expression. He laughed.

"Don't let him fool you. Under that baggy T-shirt is a lean fighting machine. Nolan's mother worried that he was too into computers and made him take karate class. Let's just say he took to it."

"Interesting. I can't say I'm surprised. Nothing Nolan could do would really surprise me. What do you want me to do with her, assuming she wants to come in?"

"We'll put her in one of the rooms down here. You can question her in the library. We have video surveillance in there because it's a common area. We can record everything she says." Tyler walked to a panel in the wall and popped it open, showing Ethan the hidden wiring and digital recording equipment.

"We should turn her over to the FBI." He wanted to question her, but protocol demanded that he call the authorities.

"Yes, we should, and we will. But she came to you. Ask your questions…then we'll call." He handed Ethan the remote for the gate and the service weapon that he'd stowed for Ethan on their arrival. "Bring her in. I'll make sure Kelsey and Janie are safely upstairs."

Nolan reappeared beside them, a small black pack over his shoulder. "To find the tracker" was his only explanation.

Ethan and Nolan drove one of the estate's golf carts down the long, curvy drive to the gate, Ethan still fuming a little that he had been tagged with a GPS without realizing it.

As they rounded the last curve, Ethan slowed the golf cart nearly to a stop to give Nolan time to jump out. "Watch and wait. I'll make sure she's not armed. After I pass you, search the car."

"Got it." Nolan disappeared through the trees into the woods.

Ethan kept driving. Viktoria Arsov thought she could make the rules, but she couldn't make the rules here. Their first priority was to keep everyone safe.

At the gate, he could see a person behind the wheel of the car.

He pulled the weapon from the small of his back and stood with as much of his body behind the pillar as possible, aiming the gun at her. "Put both hands where I can see them."

The woman behind the wheel put both hands out the window, fingers spread.

"Open the door from the outside and get out. Keep your hands visible."

Arsov—or at least he assumed it was Arsov—reached outside the door and grabbed the handle, never letting her hands get out of his sight. Whatever she was, she wasn't stupid. She'd maneuvered him into doing what she wanted from the beginning.

That was about to end. "Take it slow."

"I don't want trouble. I just want to talk to you." She stepped out of the car with her hands to the side.

"Leave the keys in the car, shut the door and turn slowly, all the way around." He wanted to make sure he wasn't putting himself at risk, and consequently everyone else on the property, when he let her in.

She was a pretty woman, with high cheekbones, a high forehead and shoulder-length dark brown hair, the exact color of the box he'd found in the hotel room. Slacks, heels and a sweater gave her the look of a professional—but a professional what?

There were no telltale bulges to signal that she was wearing a weapon, but that didn't mean she wasn't hiding something. "Okay, walk toward the gate."

"But my car…" Her Slavic accent was slight, but there, in the flat vowel sounds.

"Someone else will bring it in. Keep moving toward the gate, no sudden movements."

"I guess I deserve this treatment. You have no idea whether you can trust me. Truly, I have only your best interest at heart."

"Really? That why you ran, back at the hotel?" He looked into her eyes and saw nothing that alarmed him. Pressing the code on the remote, he opened the gate.

"I ran because once I am in police custody, I can't control the information. If I come to you first, you know what I know. What happens next is up to you."

People who traffic children deserve to be in jail. It was on the tip of his tongue to say, but he held the words in. They needed to know what she knew. She was the only link to what had to be a much larger organization. As sick as it made him to even think about, trafficking children might only be the tip of the iceberg.

EIGHT

Ethan halted the gate's progress with only a small opening. "Step through, slowly."

After she did as he said, he closed it behind them. "Walk. What's your name?"

"Viktoria Arsov."

"Is that your real name?"

"Yes." At his hard look, she breathed out a frustrated sigh. "Why would I lie? What do I have to gain?"

"You control the information, remember?"

"I see why you would be suspicious." She nodded slowly, then shrugged. "At home, I am called Vika."

"Vika Arsov?"

She nodded, but there was enough of a hesitation that he figured the last name was an alias. It appeared that she didn't want to lie to him, though, which was a good sign.

"I am sure you have questions." She tucked a stray piece of hair behind her ear. "I will answer what you wish."

"Later. Get in and drive."

Viktoria sent him a startled look. "Drive?"

"I want both your hands and one of your feet occupied. And don't worry, we have plenty of time for questions."

It took her a few tries to get the hang of the golf cart, but within a few minutes, they were back at the main house. His brother, bless him, had sent the visiting police team—in their gear, with weapons at the ready, to line the trees. Ethan knew they were only using blanks for the purposes of their exercises, but Viktoria wouldn't know that.

She shot a sideways glance at him. "You were expecting an invasion? I am only one small woman."

Ethan ignored her. "Park the cart and get out."

Viktoria sighed again. "Ethan, you should understand by now that I'm on your side."

"I think you're on your own side, but we'll see." He nudged her forward across the patio toward the French doors that led into the living room. If he could avoid a scene in the kitchen, that would be ideal. He tucked his weapon into the small of his back and opened the door for her.

In the fifteen or twenty minutes he'd been gone, the library had been cleared. His brother, or possibly Gracie, had moved the table into the center of the room.

His phone buzzed in his pocket. It was his brother, texting that they'd moved the computer to the room across the hall, where they would be watching the live feed from the surveillance cameras.

"Have a seat." Ethan gestured to a chair at the table. "This might take a while."

"I'll tell you what you want to know. I didn't come here to keep secrets." She sat gracefully in the chair, lacing her fingers together and putting them on the table in front of her.

"Why did you come here?"

European shrug. "It's complicated."

"Start at the beginning. I have time." He sat back in his chair.

"I was born in Moldova, before the Soviet Union fell. The economy of my country was dependent on the Soviets."

"I'm not sure you have to start quite that far back." He leaned back in his seat.

"Oh, but I do, if you want to understand."

He nodded, shrugged a little as if to say, *Whatever, I've got nothing but time.*

"When they left, we had no infrastructure to support ourselves. There was no work. People began to starve. Parents were abandoning their children in order to go into Russia and find work. This is nothing that has gone away. It still is happening today."

"It's tragic, Ms. Arsov, but what does it have to do with you?" Her story moved him. How could it not? But if he showed her that emotion, she would have the upper hand. And more, she would know it.

"I was one of the economic orphans. I guess my parents figured that the state wouldn't let children die."

He knew that she was trying to play on his sympathy, but if she had been through what she was implying… He couldn't fathom it. "I sense there's a *but* at the end of that sentence?"

"They were wrong. Children were freezing to death in the winter. There was only a dripping pipe for bathing. Never enough to eat. The conditions were horrendous. And when the orphans turn sixteen, they are put out on the street."

"Where they are prey for all types of predators."

She raised an eyebrow. "Exactly. I was sixteen, looking for any kind of job that didn't involve selling myself. Then along came a nicely dressed man who offered me a way out. All I had to do was come to the States and work. I would make more money than I could ever hope to make in my own country. I could get out from under the poverty that was suffocating my fellow countrymen."

He knew what she was going to say next. He'd heard this before. "Let me guess. When you got here, he said that the passage was more expensive than he planned and you would have to work for him to pay your debt."

"You are close enough. I've been working for this man ever since. At least he didn't expect me to work on my back, which was the case with so many of the others. I started out doing small jobs, but little by little, I was trusted with more."

"What is this man's name?"

She didn't hesitate. "You knew him as Anthony Cantori."

From outside, they heard a cry. Viktoria's head whipped up. "She is here?"

"Who?"

"Jane. The baby, my *malyshka,* my little one." Tears

sprang to her eyes. "I didn't expect that you would have her here."

"She is special to you." It was a statement, not a question. He could see it on her face.

"I gave my life for her. They are going to kill me when they find me." This statement was true, too. He would stake his life on it.

"Who is going to kill you? Cantori?"

"And the man he works for. I know this because they have tried already."

Time for him to turn the tables, ask the questions. "They tried to kill Janie, too. That's why we're here. Tell me who is after her."

"They tried to kill my *malyshka?*" Her hands were over her mouth, tears spilling over.

He didn't bother answering her. "I want to know who her mother is and I want to know about the rest of the children on that SD card. How did he get them here?"

Viktoria blinked and the emotion she'd revealed disappeared, despite the tracks of tears on her face. She looked at him slyly out of the corner of her eye. "You're so far from an answer, you don't even know the right questions to ask."

He stood and leaned over the table, palms flat on the surface. "Then you better start talking—or I'll have the baby moved to another location and you'll never see her again."

"You wouldn't do that."

"Try me."

* * *

Two hours later, Kelsey heard the door to the small sitting room open and looked up from the floor where she played with Janie. Ethan stood in the door, exhausted. "I can't get any more out of her this afternoon. We need to put her in a room. I can try again later for more details. She still knows more than she's telling."

"I'll take care of it." Tyler slid past him into the hall.

"She wants to see the baby. I promised if she cooperated that she could," he said to Kelsey.

"I heard you. I didn't think you'd go through with it."

"Janie may be the only bargaining chip we have. I don't think she'll hurt her. No one could fake the kind of emotion she showed when she was talking about the baby." His exhaustion showed on his face, but she didn't care.

"That woman left Janie alone in the middle of the ocean, Ethan." She didn't want any part of putting the baby in the room with the woman who quite possibly could've killed her.

"She was on a boat where Viktoria could get to her in minutes if I didn't show up. Did you hear that part?"

Kelsey crossed her arms. "I don't think it matters."

"Kelsey, this is not just about Janie, not anymore. All those children. We need to find out what happens to them. How they find the babies. Who's behind it all. And we need Viktoria to get to those answers." He looked as bullheaded as she felt.

"So you're going to use the baby, just like she did."

It was a direct hit. She could see it on his face.

Then his expression hardened. "If you want to look at it like that."

She shook her head. "I'm not going to be a part of that."

"You don't have to." He picked the baby up. "I will."

Janie smiled, patted his face. "Da."

His I-mean-business face melted and he blew a sputtery kiss into Janie's neck, sending her into gales of baby giggles and squirms. "All right, peanut, let's go see an old friend."

"Wait." Kelsey got to her feet, still glowering at him despite wanting to give in when he got all sweet with the baby. "I want to be in the room. Someone needs to watch out for her."

His jaw tightened, but he didn't say anything, just held the door open for her to walk through.

She opened the door on the opposite side of the hall. Ethan walked through it with the toddler in his arms. Viktoria had her head on her arms, but when she heard the door she looked up. She got to her feet, trembling.

"Now you've seen her." Ethan backed toward the door.

"Please." The word was a whisper, but full of need.

Janie heard the familiar voice and whipped her head around, her eyes wide. When she saw Vika, she threw herself forward. Ethan caught her, but not before

Viktoria had taken a quick step toward them, hands outstretched.

With a quick look at Ethan, Viktoria took another step forward and took Janie into her arms. She closed her eyes as Janie smiled and rubbed her face on Vika's shoulder. Viktoria whispered in a language that Kelsey didn't understand.

When the woman they suspected of trafficking over one hundred babies finally opened her eyes, they were damp with unshed tears. "She was with me a long while."

Kelsey stepped forward. "Is she yours?"

Viktoria looked at her in surprise. "No, not mine. I couldn't adopt her out because she was sick. I tried once, but she cried so hard when we handed her over to the new family that she had one of her attacks. They gave her back immediately, said they weren't prepared for medical issues."

"Where is her mother?"

Their witness shook her head. "I don't know."

Ethan made a noise beside her and Viktoria looked to him, her survival instinct shining fiercely in her eyes. "I don't know. She could've been sold, but I suspect that she is dead. She knew that her child had not been adopted out and she fought them. I think they knew she would try to escape to get back to Jane."

"The others?" Kelsey'd had enough of Viktoria having her hands on the baby and reached for Janie, who happily came back to her.

Vika sat heavily in the leather chair. "I only know the part of the business I am responsible for. I get the babies when they are born and I take them to the couple that is adopting them and get papers signed."

"Where do the babies come from?" Her voice sliced through the air.

In contrast, Viktoria's voice was weary. "Their mothers are orphans. Some of them like me, economic orphans. Some are real orphans. All from the streets. The boss brings them over when they get pregnant. See?"

"They are brought here pregnant?" A sick feeling knotted Kelsey's stomach.

A nod from Viktoria, but she didn't look up. "He works with the local clinics to find the girls."

Kelsey looked at Ethan. He motioned her to continue questioning Viktoria. She could see why—she'd had more luck with her in the last ten minutes than he had in two hours. "He lures them here with the promise of a new life for them and their baby. A job. Then when he gets them here, he tells them what? How does he make them turn over their baby?"

Viktoria's voice was harsh. "I am not part of this, but I know how he does it. Once they are here, he takes away their papers, isolates them—makes them believe that if they go for help they will be arrested."

"Then when they give birth, he makes them sign papers giving the baby up for adoption." Kelsey filled in the blanks. "What about the home study?"

The woman hesitated, but apparently decided she'd traded enough for her momentary visit with Janie. "I don't know any more."

"Don't know or won't say?"

Viktoria looked up at the ceiling, the equivalent of

a shrug. "Doesn't matter. I want to see the baby again in the morning."

"And if we allow that, you'll magically remember more information?" Ethan's lazy voice cut into the conversation.

"Is possible there is more I might have forgotten. I am very tired." Viktoria yawned and looked past Kelsey to Ethan. "Is there a room where I might rest?"

Ethan waved his brother into the room. "He'll show you to a room. The FBI will be here in the morning, so any advantage you might've gained by telling us what you know will be lost. They will take you into custody. Trafficking children for profit is illegal."

As Tyler led Viktoria out of the room, she looked back. "The young women are in the United States legally. The babies are born citizens of the United States. The adoptions are processed according to the law."

Ethan closed his eyes and ran a hand over his short hair, breathing a frustrated sigh.

"Is she right? Is there no legal recourse here?" Kelsey demanded an answer. Janie squirmed in her arms, clearly unhappy at her tone.

He walked to the door and closed it. "At the very least, we know they kidnapped my son and laundered him through their system. We know that they coerce these young women into giving up their parental rights, which is also illegal."

"What do you think happens to them after they give birth?" She wasn't sure she wanted to know.

Ethan's blue-gray eyes turned to ice. "I think Cantori, or whatever he calls himself now, sells them to the highest bidder—like my cover as a businessman. I was right all along about trafficking the girls. I just didn't know how far they were willing to go to make a profit."

"It makes me want to hunt Cantori down. And, believe it or not, I'm pretty good at hunting deadbeats down and making them pay." Kelsey lifted Janie higher in her arms. The toddler made a fist and brought her fingers to her mouth.

"What does that mean, what she just did?"

"When you put your fingers together and touch your chin, it means 'eat.'" She gave the baby a kiss on the cheek. "Let's go get you some dinner, okay?"

As they left the room, Gracie stopped Ethan. "I hope it's okay with you, but I made up the pool house for Kelsey and Janie."

Ethan frowned. "That's where you live."

"Usually, yes. But we have extra guests tonight. Another member of Brad's team came in and we have Nolan and now Viktoria Arsov. Kelsey, you need room for the baby and you need to be safe. The pool house is secure. Ethan, you can stay on the boat and be in shouting distance."

"And you?"

"There's a Murphy bed in my office for occasions just like this. Believe me, it's not the first time we've used it. The only one that's going to be put out is my cat, and he'll get over it." As she talked, Gracie walked toward the door. "Tyler left you dinner in the oven, and I had one of the girls move the crib."

"I feel like we're imposing." Kelsey felt horrible. They weren't paying guests, or even close.

"Stop. You're family. You've been adopted. At least Janie has." Gracie chucked Janie under the chin. "So go feed my baby. I'll see you tomorrow morning."

Kelsey threw her free arm around Gracie and pulled her close, not knowing any other way to express the affection that welled up in her. "Thank you."

It had been years since she'd had a real friend. Maybe since she'd been a child. Once you lost everything, it got easier and easier to let life sift through your fingers, like so many grains of sand. But sometimes—sometimes, it made sense to hold on to the gifts God gave you. And she had a feeling this was one of those times.

She felt Ethan's hand at her elbow as he guided her down the patio steps and across the marble terrace toward the pool house. And she wondered…would he be a gift? Or would he be one more important thing in her life that she had to let go of?

"Ethan!" His name was being bellowed.

He stepped out on deck to find his little brother, Marcus, on the pier. At fourteen, Marcus was more legs than anything, something basketball coaches kept trying to take advantage of, but height was not an advantage for Marcus. He ran into everything.

His curly dark hair had been clipped close to his head. He'd grown up so much in the last couple of years, which served only to remind Ethan how much he'd missed in the two years without his little boy.

shirt

"Dude! I need to talk to you." His brother was bouncing back and forth from one foot to the other. Marcus's T-shirt said *The police never think it's as funny as you do.* Ethan muffled a laugh.

"Does Mom know you have that shirt on?" He leaned against the opposite side of the boat, crossing his legs at the ankle. This could be fun. "'Cause I'm pretty sure she wouldn't find it amusing."

Marcus let out a long drawn-out sigh, making sure Ethan could hear it, and pulled a hooded sweatshirt from his backpack. He tugged it on over his head and glared at Ethan. "Better, your majesty?"

"Why yes, my loyal subject." Ethan stepped off the boat onto the dock and started toward shore. "What are you doing here?"

"I have a problem."

Ethan's steps faltered as he realized Marcus had specifically come to him with a problem, but he picked it back up. "So you're here because, why? You want me to run interference with Mom?"

Marcus laughed. "No, for real, Mom's cool. But she doesn't know anything about girls. She tried to tell me Dad could give me advice."

Girls. Ethan took a deep breath. "Well, Dad's been married a long time. Some would say that would point to him having a fairly good understanding of women."

His little brother looked at him and scratched his head with one finger. "Maybe I should wait until Tyler's finished with dinner."

"No, no—I got this. Give it to me straight up. What's going on?"

"There's a dance," Marcus blurted.

"Oh. And you want to go?" Asking a girl to a school dance had to rank right up there with shooting yourself in the foot. Not that he'd done either.

"Yeah, kinda. There's this girl I like. We're talking, you know. But I heard her say she thought she was going to go to the dance with all the other cheerleaders. And that's not chill, dude. Now if I ask her, she has a good excuse not to go." Marcus jammed his hands in his pockets and stepped off the end of the dock onto the shore.

"You need to ask her anyway."

"But—"

"No, hear me out." Ethan put his hand on Marcus's arm and Marcus's mouth slammed shut. "She probably said that because she was afraid she wasn't going to have a date and she wanted to save face. I bet she wants to go with you."

They walked toward the pool house. Marcus had misery written all over his face. "What do I say?"

"The best thing would be something like, 'Hey, would you go to the dance with me?'"

"You're stupid."

"No, he's smart." Kelsey's voice came from behind them. Ethan hadn't heard her come out, and obviously Marcus hadn't either because he whirled around. He whistled under his breath. "Whoa, dude."

Ethan elbowed his little brother in the ribs. Hard. "Manners."

"Why is Ethan smart? I thought women liked mysterious men." Marcus looked at Kelsey, giving her the hard question, thank goodness.

"In this case, she's probably wondering if she'll have a date to the dance and she might be wondering if you even like her. It's much better to have a straightforward approach. It also might help if you invite her friends to go along. It would take the pressure off the two of you."

"Is that how Ethan did it with you?" The fourteen-year-old crossed his arms and leaned back.

She opened her mouth, but no sound came out.

"We work together, shrimp. This is Kelsey." Ethan resisted the urge to elbow his brother again. The first time was obviously ineffective. The problem was, with Marcus, he wasn't sure one more would do the trick.

"Mom just dropped me off while she went to get gas, so she's probably waiting out there. I've gotta jam." He shot Ethan a sideways look. "All right, I'll do it, but if I ask Shawna to the dance and she says no, I'm gonna pound you."

"You can try." Ethan's voice sounded slow and lazy, he knew, but it was deceptive. He could still pound a fourteen-year-old. He laughed and pulled Marcus into a hug. "Go. I'll see you later."

Marcus ambled off, tossing a nonchalant wave back toward them. "See ya. Nice meeting you, Kelsey."

"He's really cute."

Ethan stood in the door of the pool house and watched his brother's long-legged stride. "He's a total pain, but we can't imagine our family without him."

His brother was growing up. It wouldn't be long before Marcus would be fighting the girls off. It hadn't been that long ago that he was a chubby ten-year-old with diabetes and a foster family who couldn't care less about him.

He'd been used by that foster family for the meager check they'd gotten from the state for his care. Like those young girls and those babies had been used. It burned him up.

Marcus had almost died because of the neglect of one foster family. How many women and children had suffered at the hands of Cantori and his ilk?

There was a bit of a chill in the air, and Ethan found he needed it. Generally, he had a knack for taking information and leveraging it into more information. But he didn't have any idea how to take what they'd learned today and make it into a lead they could follow.

Viktoria had given them lots of facts but no leads. It was hard to believe that hadn't been on purpose. Frustration built in him like a summer storm building offshore.

Ethan dropped his head. *God, please, help me to know what to do next. I don't know where to turn.*

He opened his eyes. "So, I'm guessing the munchkin is asleep?"

"She's out." Kelsey leaned against the doorjamb, mesmerized by the fountain in the pool. "She didn't sleep much today with all that was going on, so she was ready for an early night."

"Will you be okay in the pool house alone tonight?"

"Yes, you're right down at the end of the dock, and Nolan installed the same security here as the house." She ducked under his arm and walked out onto the pool deck. "Do you want to sit out here for a while? I could use some fresh air." She wiggled the baby monitor at him as she dropped into one of the sunbathing chairs.

He settled in the chair beside her and stretched out his legs. Without really thinking about it, he reached for her hand.

"What's going on in your head, Ethan Clark?"

"Too much to figure. I have no idea where to look for Tony Cantori. I had every possible trace put on him before I officially left the FBI. If there had been anything, someone would've found him, but there's been no trace—electronic or otherwise."

"I think you're avoiding talking about what you're really thinking."

"Do you mean Charlie?"

She nodded. "It would be hard not to be thinking about him."

He looked at their joined fingers, but didn't say anything. It wasn't that he didn't want to talk, but more that—with her—he was afraid if he started, he wouldn't be able to stop the flood.

"You don't have to talk about it if you don't want to. I know the last few days must have been awful for you." Her words stumbled to a stop and she sent him a look full of compassion and caring. The same kind of look that had sent him running away from well-meaning people.

But somehow, compassion from Kelsey he could

take. There was something about her—she didn't coddle, didn't judge.

He rubbed her finger with his thumb, and when her eyes skimmed up to meet his, he shrugged a little, tried to come up with the words to explain. "I feel…guilty. That I didn't know he was alive. Somehow I should've been able to feel it. Know it."

She gripped his hand tighter but didn't speak.

"I watched her die, Kels—it was the most horrible thing I've ever seen. Everything I did was to build a safer world for my family, and I couldn't keep them safe. I was still alive, but I didn't want to be."

"I know." Her eyes were brimming, but the tears wouldn't fall. "I was there when my parents died."

"What?"

She blinked and two tears streaked down her cheeks. "I know what it's like to see people you love die. Then to have to go on as if they were never there. It's like life played a cruel trick. I kept waiting to wake up and find out it was all a nightmare, but it wasn't."

His lips were trembling as he listened. With some effort, he stilled them. "Yes. It was like that. I kept waiting for Amy to open the door, walk in and make me a part of the joke."

"And Charlie?"

He swallowed hard, not even trying to stop the memory of those first days after. "I was so messed up that I didn't try to finish the case. And now I know that was the point. They wanted me to quit. I have to know why. What was I so close to finding out that they felt they had to kill my wife and steal my child?"

"I don't know, Ethan. Do you think we're closer to finding out, now that Viktoria came forward to save our Janie?"

"Only if she gives us information to move forward. Right now, she isn't giving us anything. It's helpful to know what they were doing and how they were doing it, but we need the *who*." Who would do that to him, to his family.

"We'll get there."

"I can't make any contact with Charlie until I know he'll be safe. We already have one baby in danger."

"We can protect her and make sure that we protect Charlie too." She leaned forward. "You have a whole team of people helping you. Tyler, Gracie, Nolan, Joe Sheehan. And you have me. I'm not going to let you go through this alone."

Without warning, not even knowing what he was about to do, he pulled her forward, sealing her mouth to his. He brushed his free hand across the silk of her hair.

Need crashed through him. Unexpected.

Her lips parted, she pulled back, breath quick and shallow. He'd scared her to death. "Sorry. I'm sorry."

She put her finger on his lips. "Stop. I was just surprised."

"I have really great timing." He brushed the pad of his thumb across her bottom lip, his fingers shaking. "I can't explain. You make me feel—" He tried to fill in the blank and couldn't. He shrugged. "You make me feel."

And maybe that was it. She made him feel, an

electrifying prospect when for two years all he had felt—all he had wanted—was black nothingness.

Her eyes were dark, her face troubled. "Your emotions are all over the place. You don't know what you're doing."

"You're right." There was no doubt about that. He tried to figure out how to explain the feelings tumbling inside. "For two years, I've been like the walking dead. I felt…forsaken."

"Oh, Ethan. You weren't alone." Her sweet, soft voice made him smile.

"I know. I know God never left me. I know my family was there, giving me time." He paused. "But when I met you, it was like you cut through all the stuff and just saw me. You're really good at that. I bet it makes you really good at your job. The kids that you work with, they have a lot of baggage, a lot of layers of armor built up."

She didn't move, just looked into his eyes, trying to see him again, he figured. "I guess. But you're not a job, not to me."

"I know. And that makes you even more special." He leaned forward and brushed his lips across hers again, not the "chock-full of temper and passion" kiss from earlier, just a reminder that he was here and thinking about her. Despite the circumstances, she gave him peace.

No small gift.

"I better go inside to check on the baby. I'll see you in the morning?" She pulled gently away and took two steps toward the door.

"I'll be here." He watched her close the door and set the alarm before he walked back to his boat. He checked the moorings before boarding, feeling the boat rock beneath his feet. He countered it with the weight of his body, the motion as natural to him as breathing.

Inside the cabin, the small wooden chest sat there on the shelf above his bed. He reached for it, feeling the smooth surface of the cedar under his fingers. There were so few things in here, so few reminders of a life that had been so rich.

He opened it and sifted through the memories of another lifetime. At the bottom of the box was one of those photo strips from the booths in the mall. Amy had given it to him while they were dating. She'd always had a goofy sense of humor, and she'd made signs for each photo. You. Have. My. Heart.

She'd been so beautiful, so full of life. She'd had his heart, too. Fully and completely.

And now he was falling for someone else. His throat ached as he looked at the picture and picked up another.

Amy had taken this one. It was of him, asleep on the sofa, with newborn Charlie nestled into the crook of his arm. A hard knot of grief and hope lodged in his chest.

He'd mourned the loss of his family for two long years. Two years with no reason for hope. But things were different now.

As hard as it was, it was time to move on. He blinked stinging eyes and closed the lid on the box.

NINE

Kelsey flopped back on the bed and giggled. Janie flopped beside her and put her feet in the air. Feet covered in soft fleece PJs. Kelsey grabbed her toes and wiggled them through the cloth.

"You're a smart girl, my Janie. And once you get your heart fixed, you're going to go places. You know that?" She tapped the nose of her little pumpkin and wondered if there was any way she was going to be able to let her go.

Janie's big blue eyes focused on hers. "Eat." She made the sign as she said the word.

Kelsey was amazed how fast Janie was picking up words to go with her signs. "Case in point. Are you hungry?"

She tickled Janie's tummy before rolling to her feet. She pulled on a robe and caught Janie as the baby nearly took a dive off the bed toward the hardwood floor. Man, she was fast. "Okay, okay. Let's go see if we can find some food, baby girl."

After punching in the code to the alarm, she opened

the door to the pool deck and found the men deep in conversation around one of the patio tables.

As she hesitated in the door, Ethan looked up. "Join us. We're just talking about what comes next."

She sat next to Ethan in an empty chair, with Janie on her lap.

Ethan passed the bread basket to her, the knit of his shirt pulling tight on his bicep. She held the baby tighter in her arms.

Tyler held up a carafe. "I only brought coffee—I'm sorry there's no tea."

"Coffee's fine." At his quizzical look, she added, "Whatever's handy is fine—I'm good."

Tyler poured black coffee in a mug. "We do have some cream for the wimpy people at the table." He gave his brother a pointed look.

"I refuse to be baited into arguing with you. Besides, I don't think cream makes a guy wimpy. Do you, Nolan?"

Nolan looked up from his plate. "Uh…no. Definitely not. I mean, I like mine black, but I wouldn't call you a wimp just because you like fluffy topping on your coffee."

Kelsey hid her grin and placed a homemade croissant on her plate. She broke off a piece for Janie and then had to untangle the baby's fingers from her long hair. "So, what's going on? Are we waiting for the FBI?"

Ethan looked up from his plate. "No. Two reasons. One, I think we'll have better luck with Arsov if we continue the line of questioning we started yesterday. And two…"

Nolan pulled something out of his pocket and tossed it on the table. "This."

"What is that?" She didn't know what it was, but it looked ominous to Kelsey.

"It's the GPS tracker I found on Viktoria's car. Standard government issue." Nolan's light brown eyes were tired. Serious.

"What does that mean?" She looked to Ethan for the answer.

His face settled in grim lines. "I should've suspected before, but I couldn't believe that someone on my team would sell me out, get my family killed."

"You think someone in the FBI is in on this?"

Ethan nodded slowly, catching his brother's eye.

Tyler's shrug said *maybe.* "It's difficult to swallow, but it wouldn't be the first time one of the 'good guys' got lured by the prospect of easy money. Once you're in, even if you change your mind, it's too late."

"Do you have any idea who it could be?"

"It had to be someone close enough to my investigation to know what was going on—there were only a few agents privy to the details of the sting. All people I trusted with my life." The disgust on Ethan's face was unmistakable.

"I don't understand how we're going to find this person, or people, if they've been able to stay hidden this long." As Janie reached for the table, Kelsey handed her another piece of bread.

"We've got Viktoria and Janie. We've got the photo evidence that the adoption scam actually took place. And hopefully, we're going to get Tony Cantori's location out of Viktoria." Ethan pushed his own plate away, half-eaten.

Nolan didn't seem to have that problem. He shoved the rest of his croissant in his mouth, covered in fresh raspberry jam. "And we're going to follow the money. You always follow the money. If any of the guys on Ethan's team were on the take, I can find the evidence."

He had a smidgeon of jam left in the corner of his mouth. Kelsey handed him a napkin.

The computer genius, today dressed in jeans and a light green tee with the Mountain Dew logo, wiped his mouth with the napkin and grinned at her. "We're going to take them down."

Ethan's smile was a little weak but still reassured her that he was hanging in there. "Nolan loves a good hunt through cyberspace." He pushed back from the table. "Do you think we could take Janie in to see Arsov? I want the baby in the room. I want Viktoria to see exactly what's at stake if she doesn't cooperate with me."

"And that is…?" Kelsey handed the baby another bite of croissant and vowed silently to supplement it with something healthy as soon as possible.

"Janie."

Involuntarily she hugged the baby closer. "You think she'll be in danger until we get them off the streets."

"I do. And with her going for surgery next week, she'll be very vulnerable. I want this tied up before then."

"What do you want me to do?"

"Stay nearby. We want to keep her thinking about the baby. She came this far to protect the child. We need her to remember that."

"Do you want to hold her while I change?" Kelsey didn't give him a chance to refuse. She handed Janie to Ethan—Janie, who definitely didn't have a hard time bonding with people. She fisted her little hand in his shirt and pulled up in his lap, leaving a trail of croissant crumbs on his clean shirt.

As Kelsey latched the pool house door behind her, she heard him laugh, deep and full. She closed her eyes and leaned against the door. She was falling in love. With the baby and the man.

A man who kissed her last night. And really kissed her. She kind of felt the need to fan herself all over again.

But despite that, he was a man she wasn't sure was ready to let go of his past. A man who had a lot to come to grips with to deal with that past.

She could see the writing on the wall—she with her missionary-kid history of leaving friends and moving on. There was always another assignment, another place that would break her heart.

Oh, yeah, she knew hurt was coming her way, but she wouldn't stop it. Sometimes hurt was the only way you knew you were alive.

A few minutes later, Kelsey reappeared in a lightweight blouse loose over the jeans, which she had rolled up to right above the ankle. She still wasn't putting all her weight in the right places on her feet, Ethan noticed.

But she was walking easier than she had the day before, in borrowed flip-flops.

Her black hair was in a loose braid down her back. Tendrils had escaped to play around her face. She was so beautiful. He was stunned by it, by her. Not just her physical beauty, but by the generosity that she seemed to share effortlessly with those around her. And that was what it was, he thought. The inner beauty that reflected a kind of peace that seemed rare these days.

Janie caught a glimpse of her and started bouncing in his arms. He wasn't the only one who had taken a shine to the social worker.

Tyler stood, too. "I'm going to head back to the kitchen. Ethan's favorite comfort food tonight. Roast, carrots and potatoes. With my own flair, of course. Kelsey, if you have a favorite, I'll try to make it for you while you're here."

"Chicken and dumplings," Nolan inserted. His light brown eyes gleamed in the early morning light. "With those little baby carrots still attached to the leaves. I love those."

"Yeah, I know what you like, Nolan. It's on the week's menu already."

Nolan's fist pumped the air. "Yes!"

"I swear you act just like my little brother." Ethan shook his head at Nolan, but his mind was on how Kelsey's face had gone blank at Tyler's question. "Kels?"

"What? Oh, I really don't have any favorites. Whatever you guys like is fine."

His ribs were bruising from Janie's relentlessly

kicking him to get to Kelsey. He passed her over. "Tyler doesn't mind. He likes figuring out ways to tweak people's favorites to make them more creative and hoity-toity."

Tyler rolled his eyes. "I can't believe you just used the word *hoity-toity*."

Nolan made a speculative face. "No, he's right. Your food is kind of hoity-toity. I mean, I love those little carrots, but they're fancy."

A long-suffering sigh from Tyler made Ethan smile despite everything, the good-natured teasing getting all their minds off what was at stake here, even if just for a few minutes. "Okay, Kelsey, spill it. What's your favorite?"

She started for the main house. "I had to eat whatever was put in front of me growing up. If it filled me up, I ate it. Therefore, I'm not picky."

"And holidays?"

"Pretty much like any other day. It's not that big a deal." She turned back, looked from face to face. They were all staring at her. "C'mon guys, really?"

Ethan caught up with her and walked beside her, staying on the pool side, Nolan and Tyler following behind them. "Do you make a big deal out of holidays for the kids in foster care?"

"Yes, of course, but that's because they don't always have anyone to make a big deal for them." She stopped and looked at him. He gave her an I-knew-it look. "It wasn't like that for me."

"I believe you." He had no doubt that she was more

generous with others than she expected people to be with her.

His expression dropped into serious lines, and he glanced back to see how close the others were. "Just to warn you, I have a feeling Viktoria is going to be harder to crack today. She's had a night's rest and time to think."

"I'm going to need more coffee." Nolan peeled off toward the kitchen door right behind Tyler.

"So, are you going to be harder on her?" Kelsey hitched Janie higher on her hip and patiently untangled sticky baby fingers from her braid for what seemed to Ethan to be the umpteenth time.

"No, I'm going to remind her of Janie's surgery and try to get her to talk now. We need this wrapped up. It can't go on indefinitely." His stomach was in knots already, despite the joking.

"I agree—I'll be behind you all the way. Whatever you need me to do. But first, I'm stopping in the kitchen for a sippy cup of milk."

"First things first." He took a deep breath, keeping his eyes locked with hers. "Okay. One goal today. Tony Cantori."

"You get started. I'll be there in a few minutes." Ethan watched her walk away, the memory of last night's kiss on his mind. He walked toward the library, where one of the cops staying here had put Viktoria Arsov for her breakfast. Despite Brad's earlier antagonism, he and his team had proven to be invaluable once Tyler filled them in on what was going on. They were patrolling the property, and one of them had sat outside Viktoria's door around the clock. Ethan wondered what they would do when the team checked out later that morning.

He nodded to the cop at the door and entered the room. Viktoria sat at the table. Someone—Gracie, probably—had given her a pair of sweats and some tennis shoes to wear. Her newly dyed dark hair had been pulled back into a low ponytail.

But what he really noticed was the exhaustion that haunted her face. Dark circles ringed her eyes. She seemed to have aged overnight.

She looked up at him with her pale blue eyes. "I am going to jail. Is that right?"

Ethan sat in the chair across the table from her, laying the file folder that he'd brought square in front of him. He didn't open it. He was nervous. There was so much at stake today. The library normally had a warm and cozy feel, but this morning it felt claustrophobic, the window too small for the space.

He leaned back in the leather chair, crossed his ankle over his knee and nodded slowly. "Yes. Though it's possible if you cooperate and testify against Tony Cantori and whoever is running him, you'll get a reduced sentence."

"You said they tried to kill my *malyshka*. They sent someone after her?"

She'd obviously been saving these questions overnight. "Yes, a hit team."

"I got Jane to you. I got you started looking into this because I want her to be safe. I want her to get her heart fixed." The Moldovan woman stood, paced to the window.

Ethan didn't move to stop her, instead letting his low, slow tones do the work so she could make the decision. "The chances are good that we're safe here, but I still wouldn't stand by the window if I were you."

She whirled around, fitting herself against the wall next to the window. "You are serious?"

"As a heart attack." He tried not to let his anxiety show, instead letting her see a laid-back lawman, nothing but time to kill. "You must know that they're after you. The only way you'll be protected is to share the information you have with us."

"It won't help. I'm a dead woman. I knew it as soon as I left with Janie." Her lips were tight.

"Then you have nothing to lose by telling me where Cantori is."

She slid back into the chair, one millimeter at a time, shooting sideways glances at the uncovered window. "I don't know where he is."

"Come on, Viktoria." He leaned forward and got as close to her face as he could. Maybe it was time for some shock value. He opened the folder and pulled out a photograph, slapping it on the table. "Do you recognize this?"

She glanced at it, making a horrified sound as what the photo showed sunk in.

"This is Ristorante Giorgio after the explosion. Cantori killed six people in order to murder my wife."

He laid another picture on the table, this one of a single hand bearing a wedding ring, next to an evidence marker on the asphalt. The hand was nearly perfect, barely a scratch on it. "Her name was Amy. There wasn't enough left of her to have a casket, Viktoria."

Her eyelids fluttered as she looked at him. Tears brimmed but didn't fall.

He laid one more picture on the table. This one more recent. "This is a picture of one of the men sent to kill Janie."

"He's dead."

"Yes. That photograph was taken in the morgue yesterday. A policeman faxed it to me this morning. Do you recognize those tattoos?"

The fear was in her eyes, in the fine mist of perspiration that formed on her skin. "Russian prison tattoos. He's Russian mafia."

"You know as well as I do—better—how brutal they are."

Her voice was an aching whisper. "What do you want from me? They are going to do to me what they did to your wife. Worse."

He felt for her—he did. No matter what she'd done, she was a victim. But he couldn't stop asking questions. They had to know how to find Cantori. "Janie will have her first surgery next week, Vika. She's going to be in a hospital with people who won't know how to protect her."

She dropped her head into her hands.

"Help me now and I can make sure she's safe next week. We want the same thing, you and I."

Viktoria Arsov, who had unflinchingly handed over

hundreds of illegally adopted babies to unsuspecting couples, sobbed with her head buried in her arms.

Ethan looked at the corner of the room, where he knew one of the cameras was hidden. He turned his hands up as if to say, *What else can I say?* He pushed away from the table. Maybe if he went to get the baby. If she was looking at the baby, maybe it would be enough to get her to do the right thing.

He knew she was scared. The men she'd worked for had probably worked diligently to make sure that terror was carved into her mind. He sighed and reached for the doorknob.

"I only know a couple of the names he uses."

He spun on his heel to face her. "You won't regret this." At the table, he pushed a pad and pencil toward her, then stopped himself. "Vika, I promise you, I will make sure that you are protected. Will you please write the names down?"

She nodded, and even now he could see that she knew more than she was saying. He wouldn't push her now. The names were a start.

He grabbed the slip of paper she wrote on and walked out the door. And met Janie and Kelsey in the hall. "Why don't you take the baby in for a visit? She could use some encouragement. She's given us names of aliases, but it's clear that she's terrified of repercussions."

Kelsey nodded. "Do you want me to talk to her?"

"Just about the baby. Maybe the surgery and the expected outcome. Nolan will be monitoring over the security feed. I'll get him to run these names, too. Maybe we can come up with something on Cantori." He looked down at the paper in his hand, and his face went kind of gray.

"What's the matter?" When he didn't say anything, Kelsey touched his arm. "Ethan. What's wrong?"

"This name. It's the name of one of the CIs—confidential informants—my partner was running during the operation. The guy supposedly got killed."

"Did you know him?"

"No. I never met him. I had information from another source. Bridges found this guy." His eyes narrowed in thought, but he was still reeling—she could tell.

"Okay, why don't you go ahead and have Nolan run the name? See if anything comes up after the date the operation ended. Maybe you can find outside confirmation of what Bridges said happened—newspaper articles, obituaries or something." Kelsey stooped to pick up the sippy cup that Janie dropped on the floor. "I'll go in here and talk to Viktoria, see if I can find out anything else."

He nodded, but she could see the shock still in his eyes. It had been bad enough to think that someone on his team might've been dirty, but his partner... It would be like losing a part of himself.

She pushed open the door of the library. Viktoria was sitting in the corner of the room with her back against the wall, her face in her hands.

Viktoria looked up. Tears streaked her face, but her eyes lit up when she saw the baby. Kelsey sat down on the floor beside her with Janie on her lap sideways. "I'm

Kelsey. I know we talked yesterday, but we didn't really meet officially."

"Are you her foster mother?"

"No, I'm a social worker. Ethan called my office after he found Janie. She's been in my custody because of her medical issues." Kelsey held Janie's finger as she pulled to her feet and took a couple of steps toward the woman. "Viktoria, I don't understand how—"

"How I could do what I did?" Vika held Janie's hands and let her bounce. "I ask myself the same thing. But I care about the babies and I take care of them. I think if they kill me, then they might get someone who doesn't care as much as I do."

In a twisted way, Kelsey could almost understand. "And then you met Janie?"

"She's been with me from the day she was born. I knew something was wrong. I tried to place her, but the family wouldn't take her." Viktoria's teeth bit into her bottom lip. "She's such a good baby. I looked for a doctor, but I couldn't pay for that kind of surgery."

"Why did you leave her on the boat for Ethan to find?" That was the one thing that Kelsey hadn't understood—why Viktoria would leave the baby on a boat in the middle of the ocean.

"I heard them talk. I knew what happened to him because of the baby boy." She looked down. "When I ran away, I looked for him. I just knew, if I could make sure he found out about his boy, that he wouldn't stop looking for the truth."

"And Janie?"

The little girl threw herself at Vika, with every expectation that she would be caught. Of course, she was. Vika pressed her lips together. "I knew—hoped—that he was a good man. That if he found her that he would make sure she was cared for."

"Did you think you would get away?"

Viktoria pressed her lips together. "I had hope." Then she shrugged. "These people, they are powerful. Unless Ethan finds them all, they will kill me to keep me from telling what I know. Or they will kill me for running away. I don't think they need excuses."

A knock on the door interrupted their conversation. One of the police officers stuck his head in the door. "Mr. Clark says to escort Ms. Arsov back to her room. He said he would like to see you, Ms. Rogers, if it's not too much trouble."

"Thanks." Kelsey sat on her knees, letting Viktoria have one more minute to hold Janie. "If there's any way possible, I'll make sure that you receive updates on her progress."

For just a second, Viktoria's chin trembled and then she nodded and handed Kelsey the baby. She stood and walked away, leaving the room with her head held high.

Kelsey nuzzled Janie's cheek and winced as Janie pulled her braid again. She said to the baby, "I'm very tempted to make a run for the bed at the pool house, to pull the covers over my head for the rest of the day."

Janie laughed.

"No, I guess you're right. It wouldn't be very mature." She picked the sippy cup off the floor again, throw-down-pick-up being Janie's favorite game at the moment.

She let herself out the back door and looked toward the water, where she saw him standing by his boat. He looked lonely.

She shivered. If those men were as powerful as Viktoria said they were, it was going to take every bit of their intelligence and determination to keep Janie safe and save other women from suffering like Viktoria did.

They might be facing a determined enemy, but they were even more determined.

They had to get out of this alive.

TEN

Ethan was sitting at the end of the dock, letting the sun warm him because inside he felt so cold. He'd been going around and around it in his mind. Could his old partner Bridges have been involved in this?

The only possible answer was yes. Also possible was that someone else was involved, and Bridges got caught in the cat-and-mouse game. Either way, he was going to have to talk to his former partner, and he had a feeling it wasn't going to be a pleasant conversation.

He felt the boards buckle and bounce as someone stepped onto the dock at the other end. He turned his head and saw Kelsey in her cute turned-up jeans and flip-flops. "No baby?"

"She's bonded with Nolan. Picture Nolan throwing things at Tyler, Tyler acting like a monster, Nolan acting scared and Janie going into gales of laughter. Over and over again." She shook her head, slid out of her flip-flops and dropped down on the dock beside him, dangling her feet off the edge.

He laid back and let the sun warm him.

Kelsey didn't say anything, but as a boat chugged by

pushing a loaded barge, she turned to him. "So what's up? You said you wanted to see me."

"I think my partner is involved in this. I want you to talk me out of it."

She sighed, her eyebrows drawing together. "Why me?"

"You're the most giving and understanding person I know. If there's a reason *not* to suspect Bridges, you'll help me find it."

"What do you remember about the day your wife died?"

He didn't have to think about it. All he had was the crime scene photographs. "Nothing."

"Think back. Where were you staying?"

"I had a place in Destin because that's where the sting was taking place."

"You had a crash pad?"

His amusement was faint and fleeting. "Yes, you could call it that. I stayed there except for a few weekends at home in Mobile with Amy and Charlie, when I had planned 'business trips.' Bridges and I worked out of the field office in Mobile."

"So that day, you were planning the big sting, but it started like any other day, right? You got up, you made coffee. Then what?"

"I ate breakfast at a café down the street. They knew me there as my cover." He pushed to a sitting position, shoulder to shoulder with Kelsey now. "It was routine."

"Did you do anything out of the ordinary?"

He swallowed hard, the day sharpening in focus in

Fair, No!

his mind. "I picked up the money from my team in a hotel room—we went over the protocol for the night, how things were going to go down." His voice trailed off as he remembered what happened next.

"And?"

He turned to look at her. "I called Amy. From the car. It was a security breach, but I had a throwaway phone that I'd never used. I wanted to tell her it was almost over, but I didn't. I just told her I loved her."

"What did she say?" The sun was warming Kelsey's back. She registered it, but didn't really notice, too caught up in Ethan's story.

"Nothing out of the ordinary. She loved me, too." His glance was a little apologetic.

"Think back, Ethan. Think of the hundreds of conversations that you had with Amy, even the dozens that you had after Charlie came along. What were the sounds in the apartment like?"

"Amy liked noise. The radio, the TV." His voice was distant, thinking.

"What about after Charlie was born?"

His smile this time was instantaneous, infectious. "He was always making little noises, cooing, babbling, crying. And a DVD with classical music would be on. He loved those."

"Close your eyes and replay the conversation from that day in your mind." She gave him a minute to think and herself a minute to recover. He had lost so much— his whole life—the night that Amy died and Charlie was taken. It wasn't right and it certainly wasn't fair.

He loved that little boy so much. "So, what were you feeling as you talked to Amy?"

Kelsey let the lapping of the waves against the pier soothe the disquiet in her, the ache in her throat that she knew he had to feel too.

"I was…excited. We had worked so hard to reach this point. And tonight it was going to pay off. We were going to shut down a trafficking pipeline, rescue the group of girls from going into prostitution and I would get to go home. I thought surely she would hear it in my voice." He rubbed his hands down his jeans. She could tell he was getting frustrated with this little exercise.

"What did she sound like?"

"Quiet. Stressed. But I didn't give it much thought. Maybe she hadn't slept much or Charlie had a cold." He paused. "It would be okay, I thought, because in a day or two I would be home and she wouldn't have to handle it on her own."

He opened his eyes. "Why didn't I ask?"

"Because you knew there was nothing you could do." She was quick to cut that off. Ethan blaming himself would be counterproductive. It wasn't his fault. "Hearing your voice was the only gift you could give her at that moment. Let the emotion go, Ethan. Close your eyes and think back. Did you hear any voices in the apartment?"

"This is stupid." He shot to his feet. "I can't do this."

Maybe he was right, maybe it was stupid. But she felt like there had to be something. If Charlie had been kidnapped that day, there had to be something they were missing. Some small piece. "Just try one more time, Ethan. Please."

He sat back down and closed his eyes. "The inside of the car was warm, midday by that point. I had the money in a leather bag on the passenger seat beside me. I'd picked up the throwaway phone from the glove compartment and dialed home, happy, so happy to hear her voice."

He tilted his head to listen. "No, no voices in the apartment. All I heard was the clicking of a pen."

The pen. "Kelsey, I gave her that pen for Christmas. She was always forgetting things—it was a pen, but it was also a micro-recorder. Do you think—"

"Wouldn't you have found it after?"

"I thought they both died in the explosion. The forensics team went through the house looking for an explanation of how Amy knew to be at that restaurant at that time, but all they found were a couple of unexplained phone calls. One of them was mine."

He paused, jamming his fingers into his hair and rubbing his head, where there was a stabbing ache. "Once the house was cleared, I didn't—couldn't—go back there. My mother directed the movers. She's the one who packed the memento box for me. Everything else has been in a storage shed since then."

Kelsey rubbed his back with the hand nearest him. "It's a stab in the dark, Ethan. There's no guarantee that Amy recorded anything."

"We won't know until we look." The glimmer of the sun on the water reflected as a glimmer of hope in his mind. "Come on."

He grasped her hand and hustled down the length of the wooden dock toward the house. "I just need to tell Tyler where we're going."

Kelsey slowed to a stop. "Ethan, I can't go. I want to, but I have to stay here, with Janie."

He'd been so pumped at the thought that there might be evidence out there that he hadn't even thought about their responsibility to Janie. "I'm sorry, I wasn't thinking. I'm not sure I can wait."

"I don't want you to go alone. You could ask your brother."

He leaned forward, placing a kiss at the corner of her mouth. "It's been two years. I can handle it." It might be better if he didn't have to, but he could chin up and deal with it. "Tell Tyler I'm taking the truck."

As he started to walk away, she turned him toward her, took her time studying his face. "I'll be here when you get back."

"I know." He took a breath, feeling the air enter his lungs and knowing, really knowing, that he had something to come back to, for the first time in a long time.

He dug in his pocket and pulled out the keys to his brother's truck. He'd only be driving twenty minutes to the storage units. It felt like he was driving back in time.

He prayed he could find the evidence they needed before it was too late—for Janie and for Charlie.

Kelsey opened the kitchen door to see Gracie at the table entertaining Janie with a ball of dough. At the wide farm sink, Tyler was cleaning vegetables and singing along to the country music playing from hidden speakers. She watched for a minute as Janie slapped the table and flour went everywhere.

Flour from head to toe, she was a sight. But the pink in her cheeks and the laughter in her eyes was worth the bath battle to come.

Gracie looked up from her position beside Tyler. "Come on in. The police team checked out around lunchtime, so we're going with simple and easy tonight. We're making individual pizzas."

"Looks to me like you're making a mess." Kelsey dropped a kiss on Janie's head.

Tyler lifted hands toward the ceiling. "Thank you."

His wife grabbed him around the waist and gave him a floury kiss. "You love the mess."

He chuckled. "I love you, which means I put up with the mess."

Kelsey picked a piece of bell pepper off one of the piles on the table and nibbled. "Ethan said to tell you he borrowed the truck. He went to the storage shed to go through the boxes from his apartment in Virginia."

Gracie and Tyler both went still, Gracie's eyes searching out her husband's. Tyler dried his hands on the dish towel tied at his waist. "You said he went to the storage facility? Alone?"

"Yes, he thought there might be something there."

Tyler picked up the phone and dialed it. "Matt. Meet me at Mom and Dad's storage unit." He paused.

"I don't care what you're doing. Ethan's going through his stuff."

The concerned look on Gracie's face didn't fade as Tyler untied his cook's apron and kissed her. "I don't know how long I'll be gone. You can handle dinner?"

"Yes, I've got this. Go."

His gaze tracked to Kelsey as he stepped across the threshold to the outdoors. "Arsov is locked in her room and it's been quiet the last couple of days around here, so I think you'll be fine. But don't take any chances. If you get worried, call."

She nodded. "Of course."

As the door closed, Gracie picked up the cutting board and sat at the table across from Kelsey to chop the peppers. "Tyler worries about Ethan. We all do."

"Ethan isn't as fragile as his brother thinks he is." A glop of dough landed in front of Kelsey and she slid it back to Janie.

Gracie laid the knife down. "You're probably right. In fact, I know you're right, but Ethan has been very closed off the last couple of years. Tyler and Matt have done everything they can to get through to him. I think Tyler's afraid. That maybe he'll lose his brother for good if this goes badly."

Kelsey took a deep breath. "When you lose someone like Ethan did, it's like the world drops out from under you. You're standing on a tiny piece of ground and all around you is empty space."

She stared at the window, but she didn't see it. "You can tell other people are there, like family or friends, but even if you want to reach out to them, you can't figure out how to get to them."

"It sounds like you know how Ethan must've felt." Gracie's hand was warm on hers, her voice soft, inviting confidences.

Kelsey didn't answer. She didn't have to.

"You're right, you know. It takes time to build bridges back, but Ethan has. The relationships he has with his family are strong." Gracie picked up the knife and started slicing the pepper again. "They'll be fine."

Kelsey walked to the kitchen sink and wet a paper towel, not that a single paper towel was really going to make a dent in the flour on Janie's face. "What was Ethan's wife like?"

"I didn't meet Tyler until after she died, but according to Tyler she was your normal average suburban housewife, trying to make things work with a husband in a demanding field. Ethan was planning to get out of undercover work, but then Charlie and Amy were killed and he got out altogether."

"Except Charlie wasn't really killed, he was kidnapped."

"I can't even wrap my mind around that. Ethan must be going crazy." Gracie poured a plastic bag of mushrooms onto the cutting board and began chopping.

"Keeping Charlie and Janie safe is the driving force behind his wanting to solve this case." She was sure of it. Just like she was sure of one other thing. "And I think maybe he feels like solving the case might resolve some of the guilt he feels over Amy's death."

Gracie gestured in the air with the knife. "When someone dies by violence, it's natural to want to make sense of it. And most of the time, violence can't be explained by normal standards of behavior."

"Is that the counselor speaking?" Kelsey smiled as she wiped at the flour on Janie's face while she squirmed away. A futile gesture.

Gracie just smiled, her lake-blue eyes slightly sheepish. "Sorry. Can't turn it off. Most of the time, the best you can do is find a way to make peace in your own heart."

"I found that carrying on my parents' work in my own way has helped me."

"The work you do with the kids?" Gracie wasn't looking at her, but at the mushrooms on her plate.

Kelsey nodded and lifted Janie into her arms, giving her a kiss on her sticky cheek. "Yes. It's not for the money, that's for sure. But if I can speak love into a kid's life who has never heard it before, I figure it's worth it. And maybe my parents would be proud."

She shrugged, a little embarrassed. The work she did and the reasons she did it were close to her heart. "I hope Ethan finds what he's looking for today. Maybe he can get some closure."

"What is he looking for?"

"We did a little exercise that I use sometimes with kids who have a hard time remembering a traumatic event. Ethan remembered that Amy had a pen she used to record things. She had it that day. Whether she recorded anything on it…well, it's a long shot."

Nolan poked his head inside the door, coming closer

when Janie pointed and squealed at him. "Hey, munch-kin...tickle, tickle, tickle."

Their private game sent Janie into fits of giggles again. Nolan lifted her into his arms. "There's someone at the gate asking for Ethan. I didn't confirm that he was staying here, but this guy says he's Ethan's old partner, Booth Bridges?"

Kelsey's quick indrawn breath drew a sharp look from Nolan.

"Ethan suspects he might have something to do with the trafficking. And worse, with Charlie's kidnapping and Amy's death. How did he even know Ethan was here?"

The three of them looked at each other.

Nolan said it first: "We have to let him in."

"Yes, if we don't, he might get suspicious that we're on to him and that could be worse." Kelsey wished for Ethan. He would know what to do.

Gracie walked to a painting on the wall and pulled it aside, revealing a wall safe. She put her thumb over a small plate and the lock released. Pulling out a stun gun, she tossed it to Nolan. "Don't let the baby get hold of that."

The next thing out of the safe was a Glock handgun and the clip, which she slammed into place. She tucked the weapon in between her hipbone and the edge of her jeans, where she could easily reach it, and dropped her blouse over it.

She looked from Kelsey to Nolan. "What are you waiting for? He's the FBI. Go let him in."

* * *

Ethan punched in the code to unlock the door to the storage shed—the street number of the first house they'd lived in when they were children—and rolled up the door. Here were things collected over a lifetime. Baby cribs and rocking chairs, outdated artwork. And along one wall, the boxes from his old life, neatly labeled in his mother's hand.

He rubbed sweaty palms down the side of his jeans. It shouldn't be this hard to open a few boxes. It was just stuff.

A footstep echoed down the breezeway outside. He reached behind to the small of his back where he'd secreted his handgun.

"Ethan?"

He knew that voice. And it wasn't the voice of danger, unless you counted the dozens of times he'd gotten grounded for the stuff his brothers got him into. He tucked his weapon back into the waistband of his jeans and dropped his shirt over it.

"In here, Tyler," he called, as he walked deeper into the recesses of the storage unit, keeping an eye on the door.

The light from outside was blocked by two men, standing shoulder to shoulder in the doorway. His brothers. Tyler and Matt.

"So, Tyler roped you into coming along?"

"Well, Lara had me staining and weatherproofing the back deck, so it seemed like a good idea. What can we do?" Matt, in paint-stained jeans and an old fire department T-shirt, looked at the stack of boxes with a wary eye.

Ethan had been prepared to do this alone. Had even wanted to prove that he could do it alone. But seeing his brothers standing there, ready to lend support, warmed a place in him that he hadn't known had grown cold.

No, that wasn't fair. He'd let the relationships grow cold. His brothers hadn't gone anywhere. Case in point, they were standing here ready to dig through the remains of a life with him.

"This is going to sound crazy, but I'm looking for a writing pen that had a micro-recorder in it. Amy used it to record little messages to herself. I'm hoping she recorded something the day Charlie went missing."

Tyler looked at Matt.

Ethan dropped his hands. "Go ahead and say it out loud. It's going to be like finding a needle in a haystack. And if by some miracle we find the pen, there's no guarantee she recorded anything at all."

Tyler grinned. "Hmm. You said it better than I could've. Where do you want to start?"

"Amy kept all the bills and paperwork on one end of the kitchen counter in a big pile. So there's a possibility that it could be in one of the kitchen boxes, but Mom packed everything up, so—"

"It's probably completely reorganized to be neat and orderly," Matt finished his sentence for him.

"Exactly."

Tyler pointed to a box. "This one says *Odds & Ends—Kitchen.* I'll start with it."

"I'm going to go with the idea that Mom rearranged

and look in the one labeled *Office*." Matt hefted a box off the top of a stack and laid it on a table that had seen better days.

Ethan opened the top of the box and took a step back. Even the scent of the items in the box smelled like home to him. He rubbed a hand over his mouth as he realized these boxes held memories. It wasn't just kitchen tools, it was the lopsided potholders that Amy made when she decided to learn how to crochet.

A zippered bag held not just a scattered selection of cheap magnets, but the magnetic growth chart where they'd recorded Charlie's first six months of doctor's visits.

They weren't things, they were memories. Of a wife he had loved, a child he had cherished. He didn't want to forget them. He wanted to *remember*.

He took a deep, shaky breath.

It was harder to remember than it was to forget.

"Ethan." Tension laced Matt's voice. "I think I may have something." From the bottom of the box he'd sorted through, he pulled another zippered bag, this one full of pens and pencils. He held it out to Ethan.

Ethan scraped the kitchen utensils back into the box they'd come from and shoved the stack of photos and kitchen magnets to the side. He looked at each of his brothers and dumped the bag on the table, spreading them out with the flat of his hand.

"There." In the middle of the stack sat the pen, a rather nondescript stainless steel writing utensil with a tiny black button on the side.

He picked it up. His wife had held this in her hand,

clicked the pen open and closed while they'd had the last conversation they would ever have. He clicked it. Open. Closed.

Matt, the youngest and most impatient, nudged his shoulder. "Are you gonna play it or what?"

Tyler shoved Matt. "Give him some time. I thought marriage would make you more sensitive. Sheesh."

"Me? You're the one who thought we were coming on a fool's errand." As Matt realized what he'd said, his face fell. "Oh, man, Ethan—I'm sorry, I didn't mean that."

Ethan gave them a skeptical look and let out a kind of half-laugh-half-sigh. His brothers were just being brothers, and in a way it was reassuring, the fact that one part of his life hadn't changed. His brothers would always poke at each other and they would always call a spade a spade.

And they would always be there for each other. Just like they were standing with him right now.

"It's fine. I know it's a long shot. It may just be the grocery list." Taking a deep breath, he pressed the button.

Whirring nothingness.

ELEVEN

Well, it had been a good idea. Ethan's thumb hovered over the button to turn it off, when he heard his wife's voice, thick with tears. "If you had anything to do with this, Ethan will hunt you down."

He heard his brothers gasp.

The next voice made his blood run cold. It was his partner, Bridges. "If you want to see Charlie again, bring ten thousand dollars to Ristorante Giorgio in Destin. Put the money in the stroller and walk in the front door of the restaurant at exactly 9:00 p.m."

When Amy's voice came again, he could hear the venom. "I called you to help me get in touch with Ethan. Because he trusts you. I trusted you. How could you do this to us?"

"Just be at the restaurant, Amy. And if, by some chance, you were to manage to get in touch with Ethan, keep your mouth shut. You tell Ethan, Charlie dies."

"Nine p.m. Ristorante Giorgio in Destin. You better have my baby there."

The phone clicked and all he heard was Amy, nearly

hyperventilating before it ended abruptly. Ethan took a breath, his first since the playback began.

Then he heard his wife's voice again. "Ethan, it's Amy." The bravado he'd heard when she'd been on the phone with Bridges was gone. "I'm about to go meet Bridges. I pray that this goes down the way he said it would. I didn't tell you and I'm afraid I made the wrong choice. What if you could've saved our baby and I didn't tell you?"

The tears were thick in her voice again. "I'm sorry, babe. I didn't know what else to do. I could tell on the phone this afternoon that things are wrapping up in your case. I don't want anything to keep you from coming home to us and I pray—oh God, I pray—that we'll all be together soon."

Ethan sank to the dusty floor, his head in his hands.

"Whatever happens, I love you."

Matt sat down on the floor facing him, all brotherly teasing gone. "Ethan, I'm so sorry."

"She knew it was Bridges. When she talked to me, she knew. And she didn't tell me because she didn't want to distract me from closing the case."

Tyler leaned against the table opposite him. "Are you going to be okay?"

With a sort of detached certainty, Ethan nodded. "Yeah, I think I am. It's weird but I almost feel better. Not knowing what she was doing in Destin and how she knew to go there at that exact time was one of the things that drove me crazy."

Tyler reached down and grasped Ethan's hand to pull

him up. "Come on. Let's go back to the Cove. We can get Nolan to make a digital recording of that so we can get a voiceprint."

Ethan paused on his way out the door. "Amy was right about one thing. I *am* going to hunt him down."

Gracie served him tea in the parlor. "So nice of you to stop by to see Ethan, Agent Bridges. Please excuse my appearance. We don't have any guests at the moment, so my friend Kelsey and I were having a fun day in the kitchen."

Bridges shifted uncomfortably on one of the lady chairs. He was a big man, one who probably used to lift weights before letting his muscle turn to bulk. His eyes had deep circles underneath them. He'd been burning the midnight oil.

Kelsey tilted her head, studying him. "Did you drive over from the field office in Jacksonville today?"

Bridges's eyes darted up to meet hers.

She smiled sweetly. "Of course we checked your credentials before we let you in."

The agent cleared his throat and leaned forward. "Yes, I did drive over this morning. I couldn't get Ethan on his cell phone, and since I had business in the area I thought I'd stop by."

Gracie sipped her tea, taking her time before asking, "I'm curious. How did you know to come here?"

"Ethan told me about this place when it opened. When I couldn't reach him I figured he might be here."

Kelsey knew that wasn't true but didn't argue. "If

you'd like to leave a message, we could tell Ethan. You said you tried his cell phone?"

Bridges didn't answer, instead lifted the small cup, which looked fragile in his big hand. He cleared his throat. "I've been checking into Crimes Against Children like Ethan asked me to. He wondered if there was any connection between children being sold for profit and the trafficking ring that we were going after. I ran similarities in the two cases to see if I could get any hits."

He caught the look that passed between Kelsey and Gracie because he took a sip of his tea and made a face. "I'll just cut to the chase then. I got absolutely nothing. No hits, no nibbles of interest from the agents."

Gracie stirred sugar into her own cup of tea, her flour-covered, jean-clad legs tucked underneath her like the lady of the manor. "It was certainly nice of you to come all the way from Jacksonville to tell Ethan that in person."

He met her eyes over the top of his cup. "Like I said, I was gonna be in the area. And Ethan and I share a lot of history."

Gracie nodded, blond curls bouncing. "Oh, I bet you do have some stories to tell. If I remember, you were there when Ethan's wife died, weren't you?"

Kelsey watched Gracie and realized why the police department kept her on retainer. She would be a real weapon in an interrogation, all cute curls and big, blue eyes. The wicked intelligence slipped under their defenses.

The day was disappearing fast, and the light came

in the windows in long yellow strips. His eyes, dark already, looked black in the waning light. "I'll never forget that night."

"It must've been very traumatic for all of you. I know how much agents and officers who work in stressful situations depend on each other." Gracie's lake-blue eyes were guileless. Tension wound tightly in Kelsey as she waited for his response.

He didn't answer, instead sliding a folder onto the coffee table. "The FBI in Mobile tracked the numbers on Ethan's cell phone from the texts that led Ethan to the abandoned baby. They were from a throwaway phone. Virtually untraceable, except for one number registered to the woman in this folder." He flipped it open to show a photograph of Viktoria Arsov with blond hair. "She's a person of interest wanted by the FBI in a number of child trafficking cases. If you see her, do not approach. You can call me and I'll get in touch with the proper authorities."

Nolan stuck his head in the door. Kelsey could hear Janie whining and crying. "Kelsey, I'm sorry to interrupt, but she's getting kind of fussy."

Bridges's head whipped around. "Wait, is that the— How did— I know you." He looked at Kelsey, who had taken Janie and stood in the door, then back at Nolan, his eyes narrowing in concentration.

Kelsey stepped in front of Nolan. "I'm a social worker for Emerald County and I have custody of this baby, the baby that Ethan found in the ocean."

But Bridges was still looking over her shoulder at Nolan, who looked behind him and back again. "Oh, me? No, I don't think we've met. I'm in school at ECJC, but I'm kinda good with kids, so when Kelsey put out the call for a temporary nanny, I answered."

"Why don't you go get started on her dinner and I'll be there in just a minute? Agent Bridges is leaving." Kelsey looked pointedly at Nolan.

"Sure thing, Kels. See you later, um, Agent. Nice meeting you." He left, whistling a popular tune that had been all over the radio lately.

Janie squirmed in Kelsey's arms and grabbed her hair. Gracie stepped up shoulder to shoulder with Kelsey, patting Janie on the back. "Agent Bridges, I'm sorry, it's getting close to dinnertime. Is there anything else we can do for you?"

He looked at the stairs like he was planning to bolt up them and search the space. "No. Thanks. I'll be going. Let Ethan know I came by, will you?"

"Of course, and we'll be sure to give him the file you left for him." Gracie closed the door behind him, stared at Kelsey and whispered, "That was weird."

Nolan came around the corner. "For a second there, I thought he was gonna pull a gun on me. I could've taken him, though." He grinned.

"What's your professional opinion, Gracie?" Kelsey bounced Janie, trying to calm her down before she threw a full-blown fit.

Gracie looked out the window as the agent's car cruised down the driveway. "That man is hiding something. And that is my professional opinion. The way he looked at the baby, I don't think he has her best interests at heart." She shivered.

Janie laid her head down on Kelsey's shoulder. Kelsey looked down at her. "I guess I better get her fed before she goes to sleep for good."

Nolan stuck his hands in his pockets. "I'm going to call in some favors, look into Bridges's recent cases."

The cell phone in Gracie's back pocket rang. "Hey, babe. You'll never guess who came for a visit." She listened for a second and hung up. "They're pulling in now."

She turned to Kelsey, and Kelsey could see the pulse jumping in her throat. "They found something big."

Kelsey entered the kitchen, hoping to find a piece of cold pizza left in the fridge. Janie had been wound up tonight, refusing to go to sleep. Every time Kelsey would get her down, she would pop back up and say in a pitiful little voice, "Mama?"

Kelsey didn't even know where she learned to say the word. Maybe it was instinct. Maybe it was some deeply embedded memory. But the fact remained that it melted Kelsey's heart even as it grieved her for the little girl who would never know her mama.

It didn't help that Tyler had suggested it would be safer for them in the main house since Bridges knew they were here. Even with the extra security they'd called in, it would be less building to guard if they were all in one place.

She crept into the kitchen and almost screamed when she saw a figure sitting at the prep table.

Ethan looked up, his face glowing in the light of one of Nolan's laptops. He looked sad. "Oh, hey there.

Sounded like you were having a rough night with the baby."

"Janie was having a rough night. I think she was wound up from so much attention today. That combined with the change in location again was more than she could handle." Kelsey opened the huge refrigerator and pulled out the leftover pizza she'd missed because of Little Miss Fussy-Pants. Sitting at the table beside him, she didn't bother to heat it, just took a bite and chewed. "I was starving."

"Good?"

"Amazing how good it is when you don't have to cook it." She took another bite. "I don't even know what to say about your former partner. He gave me the creeps. Do you think he willingly was a part of..." Her voice trailed off.

"Murdering my wife?" He shook his head. "I hate to believe it, but I don't know what else to think. His voice is on the recording."

"Have you found any more evidence?" She picked a piece of pepperoni off her slice and popped it in her mouth.

"Nolan's still tracing funds from that shell company, and Bridges is one of the names that it tracks back to." He sighed and stared at the computer screen. "Tyler called in some guy from the U.S. Marshals, someone he worked with on a joint drug enforcement task force. He says the guy is a straight arrow. We'll see, I guess. He should be here in the morning to take Viktoria into custody. I think we can get her relocated if she'll testify."

"But are you okay?"

"Yes." He turned the screen toward Kelsey. "I confirmed that the family you found is the family that has Charlie. I cross-referenced the tag number and date on the photograph with the date and names from the blog. They match." He paused. "I guess deep inside I knew they would. I just wanted to be sure."

She looked at the pictures of the boy with the beautiful blue eyes and then at the man with matching set. Somehow the thought of him sitting down here in the dark, looking at pictures of the child he thought he'd lost made her heart stumble a little in her chest. She put the pizza down.

"How do you stop feeling like you should've died too?" He said it so quietly that she barely heard the words, but they echoed in her soul.

Getting up, she walked behind him and wrapped her arms around him. He reached up to hold her hands in his.

No one on earth besides her adoptive parents knew what she'd survived that day. What she'd endured remained hers alone to carry. She didn't share it because it wasn't her story, it was theirs. "Ethan, my entire village was leveled the day my parents died. There is no explanation for why I survived."

His fingers tightened around hers but he didn't say anything. He wanted to know her. She'd heard his deepest thoughts, his hurts and fears. He wanted to know hers—this woman who had reached his heart again when he had feared no one else ever could.

"For me, it's about making a difference. It's in the

K now that

things, sometimes the little things, that I know would make them proud. They were so full of love. And when I show love to other people, I'm carrying on their legacy." Her voice was hesitant. Shy, even.

"I think I'm beginning to understand that. I'm not betraying her memory by living. I'm honoring her." He turned to face Kelsey. "Your parents would be proud. I don't have to know them to know that. I know their daughter."

Her eyes filled. "You're something special, Clark."

He laid his head back against her chest and rested in her arms. There was something so sweet about just being held by her.

A plaintive cry came from upstairs. "She really is restless tonight," Kelsey said, the weariness obvious in her voice. "Maybe she'll go back to sleep."

"I keep trying to figure out what we have that Cantori would want. Money?"

"That doesn't make sense. If he's been part of this from the beginning, he'll have plenty of money."

Ethan turned to face her. "Viktoria. He'll want Viktoria."

"Ethan, you can't hand her over to him. He'll kill her." She backed up a step. "Regardless of what she's done, it's not worth that."

"I'm not suggesting we actually hand her over. But we can make him *think* we're going to hand her over to him. He'll do whatever we want if he thinks he can get his hands on her."

"What about your partner? How will you know if he's in on it?"

"He's in on it. He knew all along that Charlie was alive and kept it from me. An innocent person wouldn't do that." But there was that pain in his gut again, that he'd trusted someone willing to do that to him. His mouth tightened.

"Tomorrow we'll work out the kinks." He turned his ear toward the door as the cry came again.

Kelsey sighed.

"I'll get her." He gave her fingertips a quick kiss and stood. "Finish your pizza and get some rest. I can handle this."

"If you're sure, it would be great if you would take her for a while. I'm exhausted." She sank down on the stool he'd just vacated.

"No problem. I've got this." Ethan flashed her a smile and took the stairs two at a time. Ever since he'd seen that baby turn blue and gasp for air, he'd been terrified she'd have another spell. He didn't want her getting wound up, not if he could help it.

He pushed the door open and stepped into the darkened room. "Hey Janie-girl, what's going on? You don't want to go to bed tonight?"

She made a relieved whimper, raising her arms up to him. He lifted her from the crib and when she buried her head in his chest, he had to sigh. "Oh, you do know how to get to a man's heart, don't you, pumpkin?"

Ethan settled her on his shoulder and walked the length of the room, doing an awkward version of the swaying motion that he'd seen Kelsey do. Why did it seem to come so naturally to her?

Janie popped her thumb in her mouth and closed

her eyes. "I think you just don't want to be alone to-night, and that's okay. Sometimes I don't want to be by myself, either," Ethan told her.

As she relaxed, he walk-swayed into the sitting room, flipped on the sports channel and eased onto the couch, making sure the remote was within reach. Janie didn't cry, so he tossed one of the cushions to the end and eased a little farther back, eyeing the baby. Still no movement.

Ethan laid all the way back, rubbing circles on Janie's back, sure that at any moment she was going to wake up screaming.

His eyes were heavy, too, and with the baseball high-lights running on the TV and seventeen pounds of baby snuggled into his chest, he gave in and closed them. It had been a killer day.

Tomorrow would be worse.

He closed his arms around the baby. Janie didn't have to worry. She was safe in his arms. No one was going to get to her, not on his watch.

Kelsey tiptoed into the room where Ethan still slept on the sofa with Janie on his arm. From the looks of it, he was going to have massive cricks in his neck and his arm, where he propped Janie.

The baby was snuggled on his chest, her head where she could hear his heartbeat. His arm supported her weight and his free hand was on her back. Even in sleep, he was protecting her.

And there it was. That moment that she knew she'd been kidding herself. The exact moment when she knew she'd fallen and fallen hard. She wasn't fanciful enough to imagine birds singing or violins playing or anything like that. It felt more like getting hit over the head with a frying pan.

He was achingly gentle with Janie and everything he did, regardless of his own motives, was designed to protect others. He was such a good man and he didn't even realize it. She was really in trouble here. In over her head, going down fast and she hadn't even realized it.

Shaking her head at her own naïveté, she took the extra mug of coffee and placed it on the end table near his head before retreating a safe distance to the over-stuffed chair on the other side of the room. His eyes popped open.

"Coffee?" he croaked. He rolled his head to the side and winced.

"Good morning." She tried not to look at him like a woman who'd just been struck over the head with the frying pan of love.

"What time is it?" He turned his arm over to look at his watch, but Janie stirred. He jiggled her back to sleep.

"It's five forty-five. Too early for her, but I needed to talk to you. Two things. Gracie got a call from one of her police buddies. A guy came into Sacred Heart last night with a bullet wound a couple days old. He had a nasty infection. Police ID'd him as Russian mafia, just like the other guy."

He held his hand out for the coffee. "Really."

Figuring it was safe, she crossed the room and handed him the mug.

"And here's the interesting part. Guess which former partner of yours finished a case about a year ago dealing with the Russian mafia?"

Ethan eased to a sitting position and sucked down about half of the mug of coffee. "Bridges."

"You guessed it. Nolan was up half the night digging up that information. The man must have Red Bull running through his veins." She sat back in her chair and swigged from her own mug of coffee, pleased with herself to see the half-stunned look on his face. Of course that could be lack of sleep, the caffeine not having had time to kick in yet.

He frowned into the coffee mug. "Did you get some rest?"

"Me? Oh, yeah. I slept great on the couch downstairs. Didn't even know where I was when I heard Nolan whoop from the library about an hour ago." She ran a hand over her still damp, slightly curling hair. "I came up to relieve you, but you were both sleeping so sound, I left you alone." She giggled a little. "You're really cute when you sleep."

He cut his eyes at her, a smile curving his lips. "Janie and I were cutting some Zs, man."

Her eyes were on the baby, but the words were for him. "She's had a lot of change to deal with. I bet she just wanted to know someone was here."

Janie stirred, rubbing her face in Ethan's T-shirt as she woke up. The sleepy toddler lifted her face, giving him a squinty-eyed look. He cringed. "Ooh. I know that look. That look says, 'Give me milk now or I'm gonna scream.'"

Kelsey dropped to her knees beside the sofa. "Hey, Janie…good morning, sunshine."

Ethan laughed. She sat back on her heels. "What?"

"Nothing. It just strikes me as funny, that you're sitting here talking baby talk and we're having this really normal moment with Janie when everything is crazy out there."

"It's going to happen today, isn't it? Whatever's going to happen, all this is coming to a head." She was worried and she didn't mind him knowing. There was a lot at stake here. "It's going to happen today."

He sat up and shifted Janie on his lap. "Probably, yes. I can't imagine Bridges waiting very long. He'll have to know that I'm going to go after Charlie, which would blow his whole operation wide open. He'd also know that Viktoria Arsov would be a threat. He doesn't know she'll be going with the U.S. Marshals today."

Janie reached for Kelsey, who lifted her into her arms and stood. "I wish we knew what he was going to try."

Ethan stood and wrapped his arms around the two of them. "Don't worry. You're going to make sure Janie is safe. I'm going to make sure both of you are safe. And we're going to control what Bridges does, not the other way around."

He kissed her head. "Now go get the baby some milk before she has a complete meltdown."

The sounds of a waking house drifted up the stairs. Breakfast making, shower running, people chattering.

Normal sounds of a normal day. Kelsey knew that it was anything but that.

This day had the potential to change all of their lives forever.

TWELVE

Ethan looked around the table at their small team. The huge farm table in the remodeled dining room of the bed-and-breakfast held them easily—he and Kelsey, Gracie and Tyler, Nolan and their new ally, U.S. Marshal Tom Carlisle, and his partner, Jason Reeves.

The marshal piled Tyler's home fries onto his plate. "So you want us to take Ms. Arsov off your hands this morning, but you don't want anyone to know."

"That about sums it up. We're going to use her as bait, but we don't actually want her to *be* bait."

Carlisle thought about that for a minute. "Okay. I can handle it. Who's going to provide backup?"

Ethan looked at Tyler. "The two of us are former agents, Tyler with the DEA and me with the FBI. So between the two of us we figure we can handle Cantori. If he decides to bring the hit squad, that poses a bigger problem."

Gracie sat her coffee mug down. "I just happen to have access to the best crisis response team in the region. We have training scheduled for this morning anyway. They may as well be here."

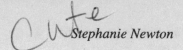

Tyler looked at his wife. "Call Todd and let him know?"

"Done." She took another bite of her breakfast. "As soon as I'm finished with my bacon."

Tyler's friend looked at Kelsey, who was sitting by the high chair feeding Janie bits of potato. "Do you have law enforcement experience as well?"

She shook her head. "No, I'll be staying upstairs, keeping Janie out of the line of fire."

Jason, the other marshal, looked at Nolan. "And you?"

Nolan looked from one armed agent to another. "I'll be running tech support. And hiding with the baby—I mean, protecting her." He grinned.

Tom took a bite of bacon, chewed slowly, and swallowed, obviously thinking. "What about the FBI agent? If you have a warrant for his arrest, one of us can stay to do the honors and we can transport all of the prisoners at the same time."

"Our problem is that we have enough evidence to prove he's involved, but not enough evidence to prove he committed a crime. We're working on it," Nolan muttered, reaching for another biscuit.

Jason, a quiet guy with a soft Southern accent, shrugged. "I don't mind hanging around. I have two little girls of my own. If one of them were in trouble, I hope you'd do the same."

His partner nodded. "Sounds good. I'll move Ms. Arsov. You'll stay here to take the others into federal custody. Local law enforcement will provide backup as needed."

Ethan asked Tom, "Do you have time for us to do a quick interview with Ms. Arsov before you leave?"

"I've got time. I'd like to look around the place since Tyler promised me a couple days' stay here in a few months." He grinned. "It looks like a real nice place to bring the wife, mafia hit men notwithstanding."

The marshal stood and unhooked his shirt, which had gotten hung up on the weapon on his hip. "Thanks for breakfast, Tyler. I'll go outside for a while, enjoy the scenery."

Ethan pushed back from the table. "Nolan, do you have that phone number?"

"The one we found for Tony Cantori's alias? Yeah, I'll get it. Are you ready to get this show moving?" Nolan slid his chair back.

Ethan nodded, but hesitated before walking away. He cleared his throat. "Maybe we should, uh, pray... before we should get started today."

Shock slackened Tyler's face, but they each stood and joined hands around the table. Everyone looked at the other and one by one, their eyes turned to him. Okay, so he guessed they wanted *him* to pray. That wasn't exactly his intention.

He resisted the urge to release the hands on either side and swipe his suddenly sweating palms on his jeans. "I'm no good at this praying stuff, something that would make my mom want to crawl under the table in embarrassment. It's kind of been a while." Ethan felt his cheeks warming and bowed his head. "Dear God... please guide and protect us today. Help us stay safe as we try to do what's right. Amen."

Scattered *amen*s came from around the circle. Kelsey squeezed his hand, nodded, her own color high—from nerves, maybe. "That was a good idea. I think your mom would be proud."

He held her hand another second. "I've got to go make that call. Make sure you keep Janie out of the way today, okay?"

"I will. Ethan, please be careful. These men have a lot at stake."

Ethan pulled her close for a hard, tight hug. "I know. We're going to get through this."

Nolan handed him a paper with a number. "The name is Boyd Macintosh. That was the confidential informant, right?"

"That's the one. Thanks." Ethan pulled his cell phone out of his pocket, watching with his peripheral vision as Kelsey picked up Janie and brushed the crumbs from her little overalls.

In his ear he heard the one-word answer. "Yeah."

The voice sent nausea spinning in his stomach. "I'm looking for Boyd Macintosh. Someone gave me this number."

"Who is this?"

"A friend. I have something you want." He picked up a digital recorder and played Viktoria's voice saying, *The man you want is Boyd Macintosh. He's the one in charge of it all.*

"Who in the blazes is this?"

Ethan didn't answer the question, just gave the instructions. "Here's what's going to happen. You're going to come to the address that I text you. You will come at the time I specify." He barely stopped to breathe before barreling on. "Viktoria Arsov will be waiting for you and you can do whatever you want with her."

"What's in this for you?"

Ethan took a breath to say something, then stalled out. He hadn't thought about that. They'd figured there would be something that Tony Cantori or Boyd Macintosh or whatever he was calling himself now would want—Viktoria—but hadn't considered that he would think it was a trade, something of his for something he wanted. Without giving it much conscious thought, Ethan said, "Half a million dollars." The amount he'd had in the satchel the night Amy died.

Cantori sucked in a breath. "I hope you know it'll take some time to come up with that kind of money."

"If you think real hard, I bet you can come up with it." Ethan paused to give Tony/Boyd time to think about it. "Be on the lookout for the instructions on your texts. And if you don't follow them, Arsov disappears."

"But—"

Ethan clicked off. "Whew. That wasn't as easy or as enjoyable as I thought it would be."

Tyler leaned against the wall closest to the kitchen door. "Now you're going to call Bridges?"

"Yes. I'm going to tell him that I found Cantori and if he wants to make the arrest he should be here this afternoon at 2:00 p.m. He'll think I'm completely in the dark about his involvement and he'll be here to get his old pal Cantori out of hot water."

Tyler didn't move, his eyes following Ethan as he paced the hall. "It's gotta hurt that the one person you

Noh

trusted when you were under was the person who betrayed you."

Ethan stopped midstep.

"I've been there, E. I've been undercover and I know what it's like to trust someone with your life." His voice was quiet. "I'm sorry that this happened to you."

Ethan turned to face Tyler. "They say everything happens for a reason. I don't believe that. But I'm beginning to believe that God can make good things come from bad situations, even as bad as mine. Thanks for sticking by me the last couple years. It would've been easier to give up."

His voice had gone hoarse. And he could see his brother's throat working, too.

"No, it wouldn't." Tyler pushed away from the wall and walked toward Ethan. "It's going to be tricky to get them to incriminate themselves. I hope you have a good plan. If this goes bad, we could be in for a world of hurt."

"If you don't want to be here, Tyler, you don't have to be. I know this isn't your fight. You've done more than enough already."

Tyler glanced toward the stairs where Gracie had gone to join Kelsey and Nolan. "One of these days I may have a daughter of my own. What Cantori and Bridges did to those young girls... I can't imagine anything better than putting the two of them away for life."

"Okay, then. Let's get Viktoria down here and get started. We've got a lot of work to do." And as he climbed the stairs to release her from the room where they'd been holding her, he prayed again. He might not be good at it, but he knew there was no way they were making it through this day without help.

They were in position, Nolan in the upstairs sitting room to run the technical aspects of the op, Gracie beside him watching the security feed on a handful of monitors. Tyler was downstairs in the kitchen, with U.S. Marshal Jason Reeves hiding in Tyler's huge pantry in the adjoining hall. The police squad had been deployed to the woods surrounding the property, not the first time they'd backed up one of the Clark brothers.

Each of the team members had been fitted with an earpiece that Nolan had dug up from somewhere. The man's resources were seemingly limitless.

Ethan sat on the floor in the bedroom with Kelsey, while Janie played with blocks. She leaned against his arm. He was aware, so aware, what he stood to lose this afternoon. He couldn't make a misstep. There was too much at stake. In his ear, he heard one of the cops posted at the gate. "Subject is entering the property."

Kelsey was quiet. Too quiet for her usual self. He closed his eyes as she laid her head on his shoulder. She smelled like a sweet mix of lavender shampoo and baby powder. He smiled against her hair.

"What?"

"Nothing, really—you're just something special. I hope you know that."

She turned in his arms and narrowed her eyes at him. "Tell me that later. After all this is over, I want you to tell me how special I am to you then."

Ethan laughed, surprising even himself. "Okay, Kels. I'll tell you then." He sobered, studying her face. Memorizing it. She was beautiful and special and precious. She'd survived something horrible and come out with an optimistic faith that he envied.

"I'm going to have to go downstairs." He leaned forward, brushing a kiss across her lips. "Be safe."

"You be safe. Don't do anything courageous and stupid like jump in front of a bullet, okay?"

"I'll try." He got to his feet as the doorbell rang. "Showtime."

He heard Tyler in the entrance hall and started down. Standing behind the door, he nodded at Tyler, who was dressed in black jeans and a black T-shirt, tight across the chest and biceps. His weapon, a Sig 226, was in plain sight at his waist. If Ethan didn't know better, he would be intimidated by Tyler.

Tyler opened the door. "Mr. Macintosh? I hope you don't mind, but I have to check to make sure you're not carrying."

"I'm not stupid," Cantori/Macintosh growled.

Tyler pushed him against the wall and patted him down, then turned him to face Ethan.

"You. I know you." Cantori spit out the word, but fear grew in his eyes. "What is this?"

Ethan raised an eyebrow. "Exactly what you think. I recently did some digging. I found out about your operation and exactly why you wanted to get rid of me two years ago. I would've spoiled a very lucrative thing you had going on."

"Yeah, so?"

"It pains me to say this after what happened, but I don't want retribution. I just want you to disappear and take Arsov with you. I start a new life." He did his best to look like he really didn't care about the hundreds of children Cantori had brokered and the women he had sold.

"While you take my half a million dollars."

Ethan allowed a small smile. "Well, yes, there is that. But really, it's a small sum compared to your freedom, don't you think? A small price to pay for the life of my wife?"

"Exactly where is Arsov?" Cantori crossed his arms, heavy dark eyebrows settling over eyes so dark brown as to be almost black. "How do I really know she's alive, and that you have her?"

"Come with me." Ethan turned and walked toward the library. He didn't check to make sure Cantori was behind him. He knew the other man would be. Just like he'd known he would come. Cantori was too full of himself to ever believe he could be caught in a trap.

Nolan had rigged a twenty-six-inch flatscreen monitor on the table in the library that he would control from the sitting room upstairs.

"Have a seat." Ethan gestured at the leather chair across from the monitor, while Tyler blocked the door. He punched a button on the top of the monitor. It flickered to life. The picture showed Viktoria looking from side to side, holding a newspaper with today's date on it.

"Satisfied?"

"Where is she?" Cantori looked at the door that

Tyler blocked with his considerable bulk. "Is she in this building?"

Pretending to be bored, Ethan pointed at the monitor. "If you'll notice the crown molding behind her...it matches the molding in this room. As does the shape of the window. She's been held here all along. I can prove it." He leaned forward and tapped the microphone that Nolan had taped to the table. "Ms. Arsov, can you hear me?"

Viktoria looked startled, then nodded. "Yes, yes, I can hear you."

This part of the "show" had been scrupulously scripted. Ethan had made the original video with Viktoria, but to make Cantori believe that she was actually here, the timing had to be perfect.

Nolan was upstairs controlling the video monitor. He had the script and was telling Ethan in his earpiece exactly what to say and when so that it would match the video.

"Ms. Arsov." She looked directly at the camera. "I have a Mr. Boyd Macintosh here with me. Sometimes he goes by Anthony Cantori. Do you know the name?"

On the screen, she looked to the side, like she would rather be anywhere else but there. Her face fell into resigned lines. "Yes, I know him."

"Could you speak up, please?"

She cleared her throat. "I said, I know him. He's been my boss for the last three years since he brought me here from my country."

Cantori moved closer to the screen, as if he could

reach through and choke the life out of her through the glass. "Ask her what she did."

Fortunately the question went right along with the script. "What did you do for Mr. Cantori?"

"He brought pregnant girls into the country with the express intention of brokering their babies into adoption." She looked down at her hands, fingers knotted together. "I was the face with the adoptive parents and… delivered the children to their adoptive parents."

"Just like I thought. She's lying. And you can't prove anything she says. I helped girls who needed jobs get to the United States, to work in the tourist industry. If there really was an adoption scam, then she's the one who ran it."

In his earpiece, Nolan said, "I've inserted a looped piece of tape of Viktoria looking around the room, but when we go back to the questions, there will be a blip. You'll have to distract him."

Ethan leaned forward. "We're recording Ms. Arsov now. Everything she says is being saved." He slammed his hands on the table and the picture on the screen jumped. "So, Ms. Arsov, Cantori here, he says he got the women legitimate travel documents, but what you're saying is that they traveled here under false pretenses— fraudulent circumstances, in other words."

She nodded again. "Yes. He told them they would be able to make money working here to support their babies. When they got here, he held them captive until they had their babies, then he sold the babies to adoptive parents."

Before Cantori could interrupt again, Ethan said,

"Ms. Arsov, what happened to the women after they gave birth?"

She swallowed hard. "After they signed the papers for the adoption, he didn't need them anymore. So, the girls…he sold them, too."

He turned off the screen. "I've heard enough. I think she can be very damaging to you on the stand, Cantori. She's very well spoken."

"She's a liar." Cantori crossed his arms, staring at the screen, as if he could reach into it and throttle Viktoria Arsov.

"Oh, I don't think she's lying. I do think you'll be willing to pay to get her off my hands. To keep her from telling the truth to the authorities." Ethan walked to the other side of Cantori and leaned close to his ear. "You forget just how much I know about you, *Tony.*"

"All you want is the money." The disbelief in Cantori's voice was enough to make Ethan question whether this was going to work or not.

"I want the money and I want the truth. You knew me as a man named Sam Prentiss. Correct?"

Cantori shrugged. "Yeah."

"Were you or were you not going to sell those girls to me two years ago in an operation the FBI called Operation Safe Harbor?"

The criminal looked at Tyler in the doorway. Ethan crossed to the door and closed it, giving Tyler his most reassuring look. From the look on Tyler's face, he wasn't buying it.

As Ethan crossed back to Cantori, he unbuttoned his shirt. "See? No wire. It's just you and me in this room.

Tell me the truth. There was a leak in the operation and you found out I was undercover."

"Yeah, there was a leak. I don't know what the operation was called, but your partner Bridges told me all about you. He was running me as Boyd Macintosh. I was his confidential informant. Well, sort of." Cantori smiled, and it chilled Ethan's blood. This man truly had no conscience.

"What else did Bridges tell you?"

The smile never wavered. "He told me where to find your baby boy at Mother's Morning Out. And Bridges built the bomb, but it was my idea to get rid of your wife to get rid of you. And it worked."

Ethan stood and buttoned his shirt, one deliberate button at a time. "Did you get that, Nolan?"

Nolan said, the glee evident in his voice, "Every word, every nuance, every facial expression."

Cantori looked confused. "What? Who's Nolan?"

"My video tech, the one who played that video of Viktoria for you, is watching through hidden cameras. He recorded every word you said."

Tony Cantori lunged for Ethan, and in the split second it took him to cross the room, Ethan had his weapon drawn and cocked. "Please. I'm looking for an excuse."

Ethan backed him up, one careful step at a time until the trafficker sat down heavily in the chair. Ethan locked Cantori's wrists to the arms of the chair with plastic restraints. "You're about to start a new life, Cantori."

The door swung open.

Ethan's former partner, Booth Bridges, stood in the doorway. He held Kelsey in a headlock, and had his own service weapon tucked under her chin.

THIRTEEN

Kelsey's pulse slammed in her throat. She knew Bridges had killed before and wouldn't hesitate to kill again to protect what he'd built.

Yet, her fear wasn't for her. Her heart went out to Ethan. She looked at his face, expecting shock and pain. And for just a second, she saw it. Every emotion that he must've felt losing his wife, grieving her, raced across his face in a time-lapsed slide show. She couldn't hear what was being said in the earpiece, but she prayed that Nolan had gotten to Janie and she was safe.

Ethan's eyes left hers and slowly raised to meet Bridges's.

He smiled.

"I guess you think you won, Booth." He let go of his weapon, letting it dangle from his thumb as he held his arms out and stooped to the floor to put it down. She jerked a breath in as Bridges eased up on the pressure under her chin.

As Ethan stood, still with the same peaceful expression on his face, Bridges once again jabbed the gun farther into the soft skin under Kelsey's chin.

He shouted at Ethan, "Why are you smiling?"

Ethan just smiled some more. "Because I've won and you don't even know it yet."

"What are you talking about?" Bridges was physically upset, his muscles jerking as he tried to maintain control over her. He didn't have to worry. She wasn't going anywhere. She couldn't risk it.

From behind Ethan, Cantori screamed, "Just shoot him, Bridges."

Booth Bridges edged closer, his face twitching. "What do you know, Clark?"

"Pull the trigger, you moron!" Cantori shouted.

The look on Bridges's face was pure, unadulterated hate as he slowly turned the gun from her to Ethan.

The shot took them all by surprise.

To Kelsey, the moment happened almost in slow motion. Bridges's head snapped back.

She dropped to the floor. Bridges fell beside her.

Cantori was screeching from his position in the library. No one moved to stop him.

U.S. Marshal Jason Reeves stepped out of the pantry, a serious expression on his face. Into his mic, he said to the Crisis Response Team, who would've heard the gunshot and would be responding, "We're clear inside."

Tyler had been knocked out by Bridges. He slowly sat up from the position where he'd fallen by the staircase. He groaned and gingerly tested the back of his head for a cut.

Ethan lifted Kelsey from the floor, cradling her in his arms. "Hey, Kels—you okay?"

"I think so." She looked up as Gracie stormed down the stairs toward Tyler.

"Oh, babe. I'm so sorry. We couldn't check on you, not without blowing the whole thing." Gracie threw herself at Tyler, who closed his arms around her.

"I'm fine." He winced. "Ow. I think."

An angry cry sounded from upstairs, but just as quickly, Nolan called down. "It's okay, I've got her. Just a momentary blip with Tickle Me Elmo."

Kelsey laughed, full and long, letting her head fall against Ethan's chest.

He sighed against her hair. "We've got some angles to finish up, like Cantori in there, but all in all, I think it's over."

"What about the girls? If they haven't been sold, we can still save them."

Ethan whipped his head up at Kelsey's words. He'd been unable to save the girls two years ago, but he had a new chance to finish what he'd started, to give those young women a chance at a real new start.

"Cantori!" He lifted Kelsey to her feet and strode back into the library as the local cops came in the front door. "Where are the girls?"

Tony Cantori didn't speak, just maintained the smug look he'd worn since Ethan came back into the room.

"Where are the girls being held, Cantori?" Ethan leaned forward and got into Cantori's face. "We will find them. And I will testify that you hid their location from me. If you cooperate it will go better for you."

Cantori gave Ethan a look reminiscent of rolling eyes. "It doesn't matter whether I cooperate or not. I'm going to jail. And it doesn't matter what you do to me now because I can't help you. Bridges called me two days ago and told me he was moving the whole operation."

"What?" Ethan took a step back.

"I don't have any idea where they are. You just killed the only person who does." Cantori laughed. "It's pretty ironic, isn't it?"

Ethan stalked out of the room, slamming his fingers through his hair in frustration.

Kelsey met him at the stairs. "What's going on?"

He shook his head. *Later.* "Where's Janie?"

"In her crib. I just got her to sleep. Now tell me what's going on."

The place was crawling with cops. People. He was about to go stir-crazy. He needed his boat, the wide-open water, where it was him against the ocean. And win or lose, his life was the only one on the line.

He couldn't take this. Couldn't take Kelsey looking at him with that look on her face. "We've lost the girls. Bridges moved them two days ago when he decided I might get too close."

"Cantori doesn't know where they are?" She followed him out the back door onto the terrace.

"We'll give Gracie a shot at him, but I don't think he knows. He's gloating like crazy that we killed Bridges and now we can't get to them." He looked out, down the long backyard, past the terrace, past the pool and pool house to the bay where his boat sat at the end of the pier.

But he'd run away once. For two years he'd run from

the pain and the responsibility and left Bridges to finish the job. And look how that had turned out. He wasn't narcissistic enough to believe he was the only man for the job, but he knew himself well enough to know he'd never be able to look in the mirror if he didn't finish this now.

He slowly turned to face Kelsey. "Where's the car Bridges drove in? Maybe there's something in there we can use."

"Nolan has his ear out for the baby in the room next door, so she'll be fine. Let's take the golf cart and drive out to the main street. If he walked in, it should be parked somewhere along there."

She was right. The car was parked about five hundred yards down Bay Street, tucked into an indentation in the woods. Ethan parked the golf cart and walked to it, dry grass crunching under his boots.

"Technically we should let an evidence team process the car." Ethan battled with himself over whether to even open the door. But if there were something in there that could help him find the girls and he didn't look…

A car whizzed by on the street. Kelsey opened the door on her side. The backseat was filled with fast-food bags and take-out coffee cups. "Ew."

"It's about four and a half hours from Jacksonville to Sea Breeze. Maybe we can find the room where he stayed while he was here." Ethan looked at the car, his hands on his hips.

"If he stayed in one. This is disgusting, but I guess

we can sift through all that garbage to find out where he went. It's like an evidence map all on its own."

"Or we could just look on the GPS." Ethan's eyes were on the small dash-mounted machine. He dug his cell phone out of his pocket and dialed. "Nolan, can you figure out a GPS?"

Nolan bit off a response.

"Okay, stupid question. Next stupid question. How do I get it out of the car?"

Kelsey watched Ethan get more and more involved in the chase for information. She knew that suggesting they find the young women was the right thing, but he was almost obsessed with it, as if he could make up for the past by accomplishing this one thing. She just hoped he wouldn't be disappointed.

Sometimes things don't work out the way you plan. And in that case, she'd learned, you have to go on and accept things the way they are, not the way you hope they will be.

But in this case they were talking about human lives. Would the girls figure out they could escape? *Could* they even escape? She had no idea what kind of living conditions they were in or if they were guarded or locked in. All she could do was pray while the real experts did everything they could to find the girls.

Ethan had dispatched a cop to guard the car until the FBI could send a team to pick it up to be processed at their big lab in Quantico. He was currently hovering over Nolan, watching as the computer guru downloaded the information from the GPS.

If this didn't work, she didn't know what they would do. She heard a faint noise from the bedroom next door and stepped closer to listen to see if Janie's nap was over already.

Nolan let out a triumphant yell as he finally got the right connection and data poured onto the screen. Ethan was right back over his shoulder. Nolan turned around. "You know if I find something, I'll let you know."

Ethan backed away, hands up. "Okay. We're just in a little bit of a time crunch here, but no worries."

"I'm going to do a data search. If he's been to any place more than twice, it will pop up. We'll exclude restaurants and coffee shops. It'll still leave a lot of places, but…" Three names popped up on the list.

"Wow. Looks like we've got something." Kelsey could hear the suppressed excitement in Nolan's voice. "He must not've had this GPS very long."

Ethan looked at the screen. "Check them out."

"Okay, running checks on these properties now. If there's anything on them, we'll see—okay. There's one house, one business, and this one looks like an apartment building. It's in red here. Let me click and see…"

He hummed to himself for a second or two. "Oh. This could be something, Ethan. The apartment building is scheduled for demolition, but crews aren't set to begin work until the first of next month."

Ethan had his hand on his phone already. "We need to get units out there to check it out." He closed his eyes. "Dear God, please let this be it."

* * *

An hour later, while they waited for word from the Jacksonville Police Department, they gathered again around Tyler's dining room table. The master of the bed-and-breakfast sat at the end of the table with an ice pack on the back of his head. "Remind me again how this guy got through our security?"

Nolan shrugged and stuffed a chocolate chip cookie in his mouth. "It's a big property. We had to reassign some assets to make sure we had everything covered in here. And even then we had some blind spots. I knew that if he got through one of the holes, there were enough of us in position to take care of him."

"Thanks for telling me that." Tyler scowled at Nolan.

Ethan walked into the room with Janie in his arms. "It could've been bad. It definitely could've been worse than it was."

"But it wasn't. We're all okay." Kelsey reminded him. She couldn't eat. Not yet. Not until they heard that the girls were safe. Ethan was smiling, but the tension in his shoulders told her he hadn't heard anything.

"Almost all okay," Tyler muttered, then looked up at Janie. "Janie, do you want a cookie?"

He curled his finger at Ethan to get him to bring the baby over. So far Tyler'd had no luck getting her to come to him. But he kept trying.

"Cookie!" She lunged forward, nearly plunging to the floor until Tyler dropped his ice pack and snagged her from midair.

"Huh. Wonders never cease." Ethan nudged his

brother in the shoulder. His phone rang. He went completely still.

Kelsey stood, walking over to him, just to let him know she was there. He'd faced so much alone. Not because other people weren't willing to stand with him, but because he'd pushed them away.

She wasn't going to let him push her away.

"Ethan Clark." He listened. "Yes. Okay, I appreciate you calling to let us know." He was quiet again. "Thank you, sir."

He hung up the phone and stared at it.

"What?" Nolan wasn't waiting any longer. He'd apparently gotten every bit as invested in the outcome of this case as the rest of them. "What happened?"

Ethan looked from each one to the next, then his face broke into the most beautiful smile. "They got them."

He lifted Kelsey and swung her around, shouting. "They got to them in time."

"Sweet!" Nolan fist-punched the air and grabbed another cookie. "I'm going to take a nap."

Gracie laughed as she picked up the ice pack her husband dropped again as he danced around the room with Janie. "We all need a nap. Except Tyler. He can't go to sleep with that concussion."

"Drat." He stopped dancing. "But that's okay. Janie and I will eat cookies, won't we, precious?"

"Cookie!" Janie beamed at her new friend.

Ethan grabbed Kelsey's face and kissed her. She widened her eyes to look at his face and caught a glimpse at the rest of the room as they all stared.

Ethan let her go, glanced around, grinned, then kissed her again. "We did good."

She smiled. "Yes, we did. Although I can't imagine all the investigating the FBI will have to do to figure out what happened with all those adoptions."

Ethan shook his head, but he smiled again. "But those girls aren't going to be trapped in that life. And that, my girl, is a win."

His happiness was infectious. She was happy, so happy, that he had finally closed the case he had started two and a half years ago, but she knew things weren't over yet.

Ethan's phone beeped in his hand. He looked at her and swallowed hard, the room going quiet around them. "It's the field office in Mobile. They're the ones who've been guarding Charlie."

He stepped out of the room to talk on the phone, his body a straight arrow of tension. He'd been waiting for this moment.

Her heart ached for him, for having to come to grips with missing two years of his son's life.

And it broke for the adoptive parents. It was little comfort that they had been scammed by some of the best in the business.

Ethan walked back into the room, his face white. "They've released Charlie and his family from protective custody. The parents want him to meet me." His eyebrows drew together, his throat working. "Tomorrow at ten."

She gripped his hand, held it tight in hers.

A half smile tipped the corner of his mouth. "Do

you think your experience at handling awkward family situations might come in handy?"

"It sure couldn't hurt. I'll be happy to go with you." In a way, he was right. She was used to dealing with tense and difficult family situations.

Ethan's smile didn't quite reach his eyes.

Janie reached for him. He picked her up, kissing her under the chin and making her laugh.

Ethan had taken a bad situation and somehow come up with a way to keep everyone safe. They just had to figure out a way to do the same for him.

Ethan gripped the steering wheel as they drove across the bridge into Pensacola, where the family was meeting them. "It's a church social worker who's co-ordinating the meeting. Someone their pastor recommended, I think. We're meeting at the First Community Church on the playground."

"I know. You told me. It's going to be fine."

"We should've brought Janie. She'd like a playground." His voice was tight, his nerves about to take over. His stomach hurt. He'd already eaten an entire roll of Tums this morning, and he was thinking about stopping for another one.

"It's better without other children. It's not your first time meeting Charlie, but—"

"It's the first time he'll remember. I know. Do you think he'll like the truck I bought him? I'm still not sure."

"All little boys like dump trucks. They like anything they can collect stuff in and roll around. Trust me."

He braked at a stoplight and let his head fall back against the headrest. "You know more about my little boy than I do. What am I doing? Maybe I should just let this go."

There it was, the thought that he hadn't wanted to voice out loud, right out there in the open where he hadn't wanted it to be.

"Why would you do that? You have the opportunity to give your child the greatest gift on earth. The chance to know his father."

"Charlie already has a dad." His lips pressed tightly back together as traffic moved forward.

"But he doesn't have you. Or his Uncle Tyler or Uncle Matt or Uncle Marcus. Not to mention your mom and dad, who will adore him. He is doubly lucky. He has two families who will love and cherish him." She reached for his hand and unclenched his fingers from the wheel, instead lacing them with hers. "Don't steal the opportunity from him by not giving this a chance."

He put his blinker on. "Thanks for coming."

"It's my pleasure. And really, believe it or not, this is not the weirdest family reunion I've been a part of as a social worker."

As they pulled into the parking lot, the playground was in plain sight. Kelsey heard Ethan whisk in a breath at the sight of a little boy running for the slide, chubby legs pumping.

"There he is." Ethan swallowed audibly. "Oh, he's so big."

"Come on, let's go meet them." She opened her door

and heard Ethan do the same. He walked behind her as she met a short, perky redhead coming across the playground. He knew from the pictures that this wasn't Charlie's mom.

"Hi, I'm Sabrina. I'm a counselor here at the church. Dave and Linda asked me if I would be here when they met you for the first time. You must be Ethan." She held out her hand and he took it.

He couldn't say anything. Truth be told, he didn't really even look at her. He only had eyes for the little boy wearing khaki shorts and a bright blue hoodie that he kept trying to take off.

Kelsey stuck her hand out. "I'm Kelsey Rogers. I'm a social worker with DCF in Emerald County." As the woman's eyes widened, Kelsey quickly said, "Oh, no. I'm here strictly as a friend."

"Come meet Dave and Linda." The perky redhead, whose name Ethan had already forgotten, led them over to a bench where the couple stood nervously waiting. "Dave, Linda, this is Ethan."

Dave was a tall string bean of a guy, but his hand-shake was firm.

Linda's eyes were already full of tears before they were ever introduced, and she didn't shake his hand at all, opting instead for a hug. "I can't believe what you've been through. Ever since we heard from the FBI, we've been praying for you."

His eyes welled up, too. "You—that's very generous, Linda." He shook his head. "I didn't know what to expect today."

"We didn't either." Dave took his wife's hand. "We

want you to know that we consider Charlie our son. He—has been since the day we first laid eyes on him." Dave's voice broke, but he continued after a deep breath. "We also know that we have to—we want to—find a way to make you a part of his life. He needs all of us. It wouldn't be fair to him any other way."

His wife had tears running down her face.

Ethan didn't think he could breathe. And then, he heard the little voice. "Daddy!"

He turned. And realized his son was talking to Dave.

He nodded. He wasn't Charlie's daddy. Dave was.

His chest hurt, his heart feeling like it was breaking into a million pieces.

"Charlie, I want you to meet a friend of mine. This is…" Dave stopped, unsure.

Ethan smiled, surprising himself. "Ethan. Ethan's fine."

"Ethan's here to see you. Why don't you show him the slide?"

Big blue-gray eyes, the mirror image of Ethan's, blinked solemnly. Then he wiggled out of Dave's arms. "Okay, come on, Ee-tan."

Ethan looked back at Kelsey and smiled.

That evening, as the sun was going down, Kelsey found Ethan exactly where she knew he would be. On his boat, where he always went when he needed to think. It was no wonder, with everything that had happened today. She'd been overwhelmed. She couldn't imagine how he felt.

He was standing at the stern, looking out at the open water beyond them. He stood so straight and tall, carried so much willingly on his broad shoulders. He took her breath away.

She stepped on board and, as he felt the shift in balance, he turned around.

"Hey there."

Kelsey hesitated before walking any closer. "I thought I'd find you here. Want some company?"

"Sure. Want a Coke? I just have the real thing, none of that diet stuff."

She laughed at the face he made. "That's no problem. I tend to prefer my sugar straight up, anyway."

He chuckled, low and deep in his chest. The sound was pure. There was much more to come for Ethan, but it was clear that a piece of him had been restored in the reunion with his son.

Kelsey cleared her throat. "I'll get the drinks."

She walked into the galley in the cabin of his boat and got two cans from Ethan's small refrigerator. Back on the deck, she tossed one to him, sat beside him on the stern of the boat and cracked open her can.

For a long minute, she didn't say anything, just let the stress of the day seep out of her. The last few days had been full of overwhelming highs and lows. The rocking of the boat and the sound of the breeze were so peaceful.

She glanced to the side, still seeing tension in his profile. "Are you worried?"

He never answered quickly. It was one of the things she loved about him. He always thought things through, and this time was no different. He nodded slowly. "A little. Everything was so emotional today. The hard work starts now. Trying to figure out where to go from here. How to really make things work with two families who love him."

"You're right. It won't be easy. But oh, Ethan. He was so precious today."

He shot a grin at her. "He was, wasn't he?"

They sat in silence a few more minutes. The sun was a giant, glowing orange ball in the west. It sank farther toward the water every second, sending ribbons of multicolored light sparkling across the surface.

"Ethan, I love you." She blurted it, and immediately wished she could take it back.

As still as he was by habit, he went even more still. She fought nervous laughter back and instead just spoke all the things she'd been feeling. "I know it's irrational because we've known each other such a short time, but that's just the way my heart works."

Kelsey could see the beginnings of panic on his face. He wasn't ready to hear this, and she'd gone and blundered into it, committing to a path she couldn't come back from. But it was the truth, no matter how silly it sounded when she said it out loud.

She forced herself to finish out the thought. "I told you about my childhood."

He nodded.

"Losing everyone like that, it changes you. But it wasn't the only time I lost a person I cared about. It wasn't even the first time. In the mission field, goodbyes are just part of life."

Ethan reached for her hand. "That must've been a hard lesson to learn as a young person."

"What I learned was never to wait—always tell the people you love how you feel. You might not have another chance." She stared out at the water, where a pelican was diving for his dinner. "So there you go."

Dusk eased over the edge of evening into darkness, and his voice was as soft as the sky around them. "You don't have to worry about never seeing me again, Kels."

She shook her head, a lump in her throat, tears welling in her eyes despite her best effort to keep them away. "I've lost so many people I love. I don't wait anymore."

He looked at their linked fingers, rubbed his thumb over hers, sighed. "You know I care about you."

She turned away from him. "Okay, you can stop now. Wow. Those are the words a girl dreams of hearing."

When she tried to get up, it was his hand on her arm that stopped her. "Kelsey, you've changed my life. Brought me back to a world that I wasn't sure existed for me anymore."

"I sense a *but* coming." And she didn't want to hear it. She really didn't want to hear it. *Check, please?*

He gave her a look that spoke volumes of heartache. "I wish things were different, that I was at a different place, I really do. But now I've got Charlie in my life, and things are so uncertain. The only certain thing is that my life is about to make a radical change."

He smiled, but it was a sad smile. "You and I come

at life from such a different reality—when you would seize love because of uncertainty, I run from it."

"But if you know that—Ethan, you don't have to go through this on your own. I want to go through it with you."

"Maybe it's better if I do this alone. I'm so sorry, Kelsey. I wish that I could be the man that you need me to be."

Her eyes spilled over—stupid, stupid tears—but she didn't give in, not yet. "Don't be sorry. I understand that you've had a lot to come to grips with."

And she did understand. She just didn't want to. She framed his face with her hands, allowing herself this one moment of indulgence to memorize his face, the strong jaw, the place where his hair brushed his neck.

He closed his eyes.

She stood and easily leaped to the dock. She waited there a minute until he opened his eyes again. "For the record, Ethan, I think you're wrong. I think God has a bigger plan for us than you can even imagine."

She could feel his eyes on her back as she walked away.

FOURTEEN

Six weeks later

Kelsey tied Janie's hoodie tighter around her chubby little cheeks. "Mama, swing!"

"Okay, pumpkin. Ready?" Janie nodded and Kelsey gave her a big push in the baby swing at the park, loving the way her little girl could laugh and squeal with full abandon. Kelsey didn't have to worry anymore that she would have an episode.

While Janie would always have to be followed by cardiologists and might have more surgeries ahead of her, she would, with God's help, have a long, happy life.

Kelsey tickled Janie's feet as she came back toward her and then pushed her again.

Out of the corner of her eye, she caught a glimpse of a dad with a stroller turning the corner into the park. Her breath lodged in her throat as she realized it was Ethan. She hadn't seen him since she'd left the bed-and-breakfast the night after their talk on the boat.

He'd sent Janie a stuffed animal and some balloons

after her surgery. The nurses said he'd called every day to check on Janie, too, but she hadn't talked to him. She hadn't wanted to. She wanted him to have the opportunity to figure things out on his own. If he wanted to talk to her, he knew where to find her.

As he walked closer, she could see that his face was relaxed, at ease. She'd never seen him like that. He stopped a few feet away, stuffed his hands in his pockets against the stiff, salty ocean breeze. "Hi, Kelsey."

Her chin trembled as she tried to control the flood of emotion that she felt seeing him again. She'd expected the love—what she hadn't expected was the worry, exasperation, wonder of the last six weeks to come out all at once. "I have so many questions, I don't even know where to start."

He smiled, a full-out grin. Kelsey stopped, almost dazzled by it.

She turned back to Janie and pushed. "You got custody of Charlie?"

Hearing his name, Charlie wiggled in the stroller. "Ethan, wanna swing!"

Ethan unbuckled his son and lifted him into his arms. "Right now we're just doing visits, trying to figure things out. They're good people."

"Mama, swing!" Janie kicked her feet in the little panda bear shoes that Kelsey bought her.

"How about a cracker?" Kelsey reached into the pocket of her turquoise blue peacoat and pulled out a plastic bag of animal crackers, offering one to Janie and one to Charlie.

When he took the cracker, she said, "Hey Charlie, I'm Ethan's friend, Kelsey."

Charlie was unimpressed, but took the animal cracker anyway, blinking big blue eyes at her.

Ethan slid him into the swing next to Janie and gave him a big push. When Janie came back toward him, he grabbed her feet, pressing snorty kisses to the bottoms of them.

Kelsey laughed at her reaction. And his, when he turned to her. Tears in his eyes.

"She looks beautiful. So healthy." He rubbed his nose with the back of his hand and laughed at himself. "I thought I was ready for this. I'm not sure I'd ever be ready."

She put her hand on his arm. "It's okay. I'm a little overwhelmed, too."

He pushed both the kids again, while Kelsey stood with her chilly hands deep in the pockets of her coat.

"I heard you quit your job," he said without looking at her.

"I'm working as a church social worker. I needed more regular and more flexible hours. I'm adopting her, Ethan."

The look on his face, in his blue eyes, was tender, but he wasn't looking at his son, he was looking at her. And she wanted to reach out to him, but she couldn't. She had more to think about now. More than just her own heart. She had Janie's to think about, too. "So you're just out for a walk in the park?"

"Actually, no. We're here to see you."

Her heart wanted to believe him. Her head, though… her head wasn't quite ready to take that trip.

Janie squealed and kicked her feet. She'd bloomed in the weeks she'd lived with Kelsey. He gave each of the toddlers a push in the swing and reached under the stroller for the pink roses he'd placed there earlier. "I wasn't wrong to take the time, Kels—I was a mess. But the feelings I had for you, those were real."

She took the flowers, lowered her face into the blooms and closed her eyes. He didn't breathe.

That she would turn him away suddenly seemed a very real possibility.

But she opened her eyes and what he saw in them… He could breathe again. "You said you thought God had bigger plans in mind for us. Would that possibly include Thanksgiving with the Clark clan and Friday playdates in the park?"

Kelsey laughed. "I think that can be arranged."

He cupped her face in his hands, her cheeks cool in the crisp breeze. His breath caught. "You said once that you didn't wait to say I love you. I don't want to wait anymore. I want to say it now and I want to say it every day, for as long as I have to say it. I love you, Kelsey."

She tilted her face up to his, and the love in her eyes nearly bowled him over. He never thought he would get a second chance at forever, but here she was offering it to him.

"I love you, too, Ethan."

Leaning forward, he captured her mouth with his. His arms circled around her and he lifted her, swinging her around. She laughed and he looked up into her beautiful, expressive eyes. "Every day. Always."

Her arms were around his neck, and though she was smiling, tears formed in her eyes. They were two damaged people, but somehow they had managed to make something beautiful out of it. She let her forehead fall to his. A moment, two, as he thanked God that he was standing here with her in his arms.

"Mama!" Janie squealed.

Kelsey laughed.

And he knew as he heard her laughter, forever couldn't possibly be long enough.

EPILOGUE

Ethan opened the car door. Charlie had already unbuckled his car seat and barreled through the open door toward Ethan's mom. "Mimi!"

Janie screamed in her car seat on the other side of the car. "Out!"

"I'm coming. Cool your jets, Priss." Kelsey, in jeans and a pretty white blouse, unbuckled her daughter and released her on the Clark family.

"Are you sure they're ready for this?" she asked Ethan. Her long black hair blew in the breeze like a flag as she reached to the floorboard for the food. She turned just in time to see Ethan's mom reach Charlie and Janie, enveloping them in a hug. And she laughed. "Never mind, I can see your mom is totally ready."

Charlie gave Mimi a kiss on the cheek and then ran on to Marcus, slapping his hand in a manly high-five. "Jump on the trampoline, Marcus."

Marcus picked up his small nephew and threw him over his shoulder like a sack of potatoes. Charlie screamed with laughter as he jiggled across the yard.

A car pulled in behind them. Dave parked and got

out, coming around to open the door for Linda. She opened the back door and lifted out an infant car seat, covered with a pink blanket.

"Oh, the baby!" Kelsey started for the car, but Ethan got there first.

"Look how little she is—Charlie couldn't stop talking all weekend about his new baby sister and how cute 'her wittle ears are.'" Ethan took the cooler that Dave handed him out of the back seat.

"That's really funny. The day we brought her home, he was pretty sure he wanted to send her back." But Dave beamed, talking about his two kids.

Bethanne Clark walked toward them, balancing Janie on her hip. "I was beginning to wonder if you guys were going to make it."

"Ethan had to do his hair," Kelsey teased. "He was twenty minutes late picking me up."

Bethanne shook her head. "He was always the one making us late for church. He used to press creases in his jeans."

"Mom…"

"He was always the goody-goody, too. Never let us have any fun." Matt came up behind Kelsey and grabbed his soon-to-be sister-in-law in a bear hug.

She grinned at Ethan. "Oh, I can totally believe that."

"Thanks a lot, Matt." Ethan snagged the hash brown potato casserole from midair before Matt could send it flying, too.

Matt kept his arm around Kelsey as they walked toward the backyard. Ethan pushed him away with one hand and looped his arm around her waist. "Go hug your own woman."

Matt shoved him back. "I think I will."

"Hands to yourselves, boys," Bethanne said, but she was smiling. "We've got a couple of tables set up for food and one really long table for us to sit at. I put a high chair at one end for this one."

She nuzzled one of Janie's cheeks and laughed out loud when Janie grabbed both of hers and gave her an open-mouthed smack. "I know. I love you too, Janie, you darling."

Ethan could tell how happy his mom was to have them all here. It was the first time in a long time. There was a bittersweet pang—but he figured there always would be—that Amy wasn't here. But today was about celebrating the living. Being thankful for what God has blessed you with. And he was thankful—so, so thankful.

His sister-in-law, Lara, the EMT, was standing guard as Marcus played popcorn on the trampoline with Charlie. Matt grabbed her from behind and kissed her on the neck—taking Ethan's advice, he saw.

Ethan's dad, Reid, was at the smoker, wearing an apron that said Big Turkey. Tyler, beside him, giving Dad pointers—which Dad was clearly ignoring—had a matching one that said Turkey in Training. Ethan rolled his eyes.

Pastor Jake and his wife, Chloe, were sitting with Gracie on a quilt under one of the big oak trees in the backyard. His mom hadn't put Janie down yet, so he grabbed Kelsey's hand and pulled her over to Jake. "We're ready when you are."

Jake looked confused. "I thought we were going to wait until after the Thanksgiving meal."

"We are." Kelsey looked up at him. "We were?"

Ethan nodded. "I don't want to wait."

Tears formed once again in Kelsey's eyes. Just when she thought she couldn't be surprised by Ethan anymore, he showed another, deeper, more romantic side.

Jake shrugged. "Okay." He lifted his fingers to his mouth and whistled. "Hey, everyone, come over here for a minute."

The entire group, even Ethan's dad, in his Big Turkey apron, gathered around. Jake spoke first. "Ethan and Kelsey asked me to join you today because all of you are the most important people in their lives. And they would like you to be witnesses as they are joined in marriage."

Ethan's mom gasped. Marcus laughed.

They stood under the ancient oak tree that had thrived in the sandy soil, through years of drought and years of plenty, surviving hurricanes and tropical storms. Somehow it seemed fitting that here was where they would be saying their vows.

Jake began the vows, but didn't get far before they were interrupted.

"Mama!" Janie yelled from Bethanne's arms.

Kelsey laughed. She was a mama, now, and the children were a part of their lives. She looked at Ethan and shrugged. He smiled into her eyes and took Janie from his mom, hitching her high onto one arm.

He reached for Kelsey's hand again. Jake continued, but another little voice cut through.

"Dad?" Charlie's voice piped up from the back of the group, where Marcus had him on his shoulders so he could see. "Hey, Dad! Marcus says you're getting married."

Ethan laughed and jerked his head. Marcus put Charlie on the ground and he ran for them. Kelsey picked him up and they stood, the four of them, Ethan's arms encircling her and their children as they finished their vows and exchanged the rings.

With the dapply light shining on them through the leaves of the old oak tree, and their family all around them, Kelsey's heart was so full. It was perfect.

Pastor Jake smiled and spoke louder. "Now that Kelsey and Ethan have given themselves each to the other and have declared the same by the joining of hands and the giving of rings, I pronounce them husband and wife. Ethan?"

Kelsey didn't wait for permission. She gave Ethan a smacking kiss, sending his three brothers into gales of laughter and whooping high-fives.

Ethan laughed. "I've been waiting for that part all day."

He wrapped his free arm around her and pulled her closer so he could whisper in her ear. "Forever can't start soon enough for me."

* * * * *

Dear Reader,

When I started *The Baby's Bodyguard*, I knew the basics. I knew that Kelsey and Ethan had both suffered a terrible loss, and that they both had some lessons to learn along the way to love.

I didn't know that human trafficking is a huge and growing problem worldwide, including in the United States. The suspense in this story is fictional, but the truth is that children are bought and sold as commodities every day.

Here's another truth: Love wins in the end. It's the happily ever after that we all seek.

For more information or to contact me, please go to www.stephanienewtonbooks.com. I'd love to hear from you.

Blessings,

Stephanie Newton

Questions for Discussion

1. What would you think if you found a baby in an unlikely place?

2. How did Ethan respond to the grief when he lost his wife?

3. Why do you think guilt was a factor in Ethan's grief?

4. Ethan's brother thinks he might be invested in saving Kelsey and Janie because he's trying for a do-over. What do you think his motivation is?

5. How does Kelsey respond differently (than Ethan) to the loss of her parents?

6. What are some of Kelsey's qualities that draw Ethan to her, despite the tense situation?

7. What are some of Ethan's qualities that draw Kelsey to him?

8. Loyalty and betrayal both play a part in this story. Who are the characters that embody these traits? Why?

9. Why do you think it takes Kelsey so long to tell Ethan about her village being destroyed?

10. Ethan worries about meeting the couple who has been his son's parents for the past two years. How do they put him at ease?

11. Ethan tells Kelsey that he's afraid of love, of uncertainty. Do you think he was right to take the time to think?

12. Kelsey tells Ethan that he's wrong—God has much bigger plans for them. Do you think sometimes God has plans for us and we think too small? How?

13. Ethan comes back to Kelsey with his heart in his hands. Have you ever had someone come to you asking for forgiveness? How did you respond? How do you think God wants us to respond?

8-13-1938
2-23-1939

INSPIRATIONAL

Inspirational romances to warm your heart & soul.

SUSPENSE

TITLES AVAILABLE NEXT MONTH

Available September 13, 2011

REQUEST YOUR FREE BOOKS!

2 FREE RIVETING INSPIRATIONAL NOVELS
PLUS 2 FREE MYSTERY GIFTS

SUSPENSE

YES! Please send me 2 FREE Love Inspired® Suspense novels and my 2 FREE mystery gifts (gifts are worth about $10). After receiving them, if I don't wish to receive any more books, I can return the shipping statement marked "cancel". If I don't cancel, I will receive 4 brand-new novels every month and be billed just $4.49 per book in the U.S. or $4.99 per book in Canada. That's a saving of at least 22% off the cover price. It's quite a bargain! Shipping and handling is just 50¢ per book in the U.S. and 75¢ per book in Canada.* I understand that accepting the 2 free books and gifts places me under no obligation to buy anything. I can always return a shipment and cancel at any time. Even if I never buy another book, the two free books and gifts are mine to keep forever.

123/323 IDN FEHR

Name	(PLEASE PRINT)	
Address		Apt. #
City	State/Prov.	Zip/Postal Code

Signature (if under 18, a parent or guardian must sign)

Mail to the **Reader Service:**
IN U.S.A.: P.O. Box 1867, Buffalo, NY 14240-1867
IN CANADA: P.O. Box 609, Fort Erie, Ontario L2A 5X3

Not valid for current subscribers to Love Inspired Suspense books.

**Are you a subscriber to Love Inspired Suspense
and want to receive the larger-print edition?
Call 1-800-873-8635 or visit www.ReaderService.com.**

* Terms and prices subject to change without notice. Prices do not include applicable taxes. Sales tax applicable in N.Y. Canadian residents will be charged applicable taxes. Offer not valid in Quebec. This offer is limited to one order per household. All orders subject to credit approval. Credit or debit balances in a customer's account(s) may be offset by any other outstanding balance owed by or to the customer. Please allow 4 to 6 weeks for delivery. Offer available while quantities last.

Your Privacy—The Reader Service is committed to protecting your privacy. Our Privacy Policy is available online at www.ReaderService.com or upon request from the Reader Service.

We make a portion of our mailing list available to reputable third parties that offer products we believe may interest you. If you prefer that we not exchange your name with third parties, or if you wish to clarify or modify your communication preferences, please visit us at www.ReaderService.com/consumerchoice or write to us at Reader Service Preference Service, P.O. Box 9062, Buffalo, NY 14269. Include your complete name and address.

When private eye Skylar Grady is kidnapped and abandoned in the Arizona desert, she knows her investigation has someone scared enough to kill. Tracker Jonas Sampson finds her—but can he keep her safe? Read on for a sneak preview of LONE DEFENDER by Shirlee McCoy, from her HEROES FOR HIRE series.

"The storm isn't the only thing I'm worried about." He didn't slow, and she had no choice but to try to keep up.

"What do you mean?"

"I've seen camp fires the past couple of nights. You said someone drove you out here and left you—"

"I'm not just saying it. It happened."

"A person who goes to that kind of effort probably isn't going to sit around hoping that you're dead."

"You think a killer is on our trail?"

"I think there's a possibility. Conserve your energy. You may need it before the night is over."

"I still think—"

"Shh." He slid his palm up her arm, the warning in his touch doing more than words to keep her silent. She waited, ears straining for some sign that they weren't alone.

Nothing but dead quiet, and a stillness that filled Skylar with dread.

A soft click broke the silence.

She was on the ground before she could think, Jonas right beside her.

She turned her head, met his eyes.

"That was a gun safety."

He pressed a finger to her lips, pulled something from beneath his jacket.

A Glock.

They weren't completely helpless, then.

He wasn't, at least.

She felt a second of relief, and then Jonas was gone, and she was alone again.

Alone, cowering on the desert floor, waiting to be picked off by an assassin's bullet.

No way. There was absolutely no way she was going to die without a fight.

A soft shuffle came from her left, and she stilled as a shadow crept toward her. She launched herself toward him, realizing her weakness as she barreled into the man's chest, bounced backward, landed hard. She barely managed to dive to the left as the man aimed a pistol, pulled the trigger. The bullet slammed into the ground a foot from where she'd been, and she was up again.

Fight or die.

It was as simple as that.

Don't miss LONE DEFENDER by Shirlee McCoy, available September 2011 from Love Inspired Suspense.

Gaining the confidence of widow Savannah Elliott could help undercover agent Trent Mueller derail a plot to sabotage the U.S. war machine. With so many lives at stake, he can't afford to feel guilt at his deception…nor should he find himself captivated by Savannah. Can love withstand the ultimate test of loyalty?

Courting the Enemy

RENEE RYAN

Available September wherever books are sold.